EARLY PRAISE FOR
ALWAYS ONE MISTAKE

"Ace Boggess's debut, *Always One Mistake*, is a triumph. Tales of gods, gamblers, and graves offer a fresh look at the human condition and the people who embody it at its most poignant."

—A.A. Balaskovits, author of *Strange Folk You'll Never Meet* and *Magic for Unlucky Girls*

"Ace Boggess's spare, bracing stories mine his characters' hardscrabble lives to hit rich veins of humor, desperation, regret, absurdity, pathos, and even a bit of grace."

—Ho Lin, author of *China Girl*

"In an age of slick, lifeless flash and micro fiction, it's nice to read a story. A proper story. A story told by a narrator who isn't overly concerned with his or her own cleverness. A story with vivid characters and surprises and even twists and revelations. A story you can smell, feel, hear and see. Those of us who know Boggess the poet might not think of him as a writer of those stories, but his new book, *Always One Mistake*, is a collection of just such rarities. It seems that, between poems, Boggess has been quietly writing and publishing mysterious, darkly humorous, vividly realized, and highly developed stories that are a joy to read."

—Steve Lambert, author of *Philisteens* and *The Patron Saint of Birds*

ALWAYS ONE MISTAKE

RIZE

ACE BOGGESS

Always One Mistake
Text copyright © 2026 Ace Boggess
Edited by Lisa Diane Kastner
Author photo by Grace Welch

All rights reserved.
Published in North America and Europe by Running Wild Press. Visit Running Wild Press at www.runningwildpublishing.com. Educators, librarians, book clubs (as well as the eternally curious), go to www.runningwildpublishing.com.

Paperback ISBN: 978-1-963869-46-0
eBook ISBN: 978-1-963869-41-5

OTHER BOOKS BY THIS AUTHOR

Prose

States or Mercy

A Song Without a Melody

Poetry

Escape Envy

Misadventure

I Have Lost the Art of Dreaming It So

Ultra Deep Field

The Prisoners

The Beautiful Girl Whose Wish Was Not Fulfilled

*for Jeff Carter, Savannah Dudley, Sarena Fox
and all my friends who've been there*

8

CONTENTS

The Lie of the Stones	13
Know Your Killer	23
Whitebriar	33
Pursuing the Fix	57
Jericho Riley's Luck	71
The God-Maker	83
I'm Sorry	103
Always One Mistake	111
The Burglar	123
Up Yours	137
The Last Time I Saw Logan	149
The Police Artist's Sketch	165
Busted Straight	191
American Toad	201
Colorful Aliens	217

ACKNOWLEDGMENTS

The author wishes to thank the following publications in which these stories first appeared, sometimes in slightly different forms:

The Belmont Story Review: "Colorful Aliens"
Coe Review: "The Lie of the Stones"
Cossack Review: "Always One Mistake"
Duende: "Pursuing the Fix"
Flyway: "American Toad"
Lumina: "The Last Time I Saw Logan"
Nebo: "I'm Sorry"
New Plains Review: "The Burglar"
Notre Dame Review: "Whitebriar"
Pacifica Literary Review: "The Police Artist's Sketch"
The Sonder Review: "Up Yours"
Soundings Review: "Jericho Riley's Luck"
The Stockholm Review of Literature: "Know Your Killer"
Superstition Review: "Busted Straight"
Tulane Review: "The God-Maker"

"Whitebriar" first appeared in *Notre Dame Review* Issue No. 41, Winter/Spring, 2016.

THE LIE OF THE STONES

H E COULDN'T TELL IF it were a hillock or another grave. Bernard stepped up the slight rise, black shoes digging into the mud and wet grass. Streaks of brown already coated the legs of his ashen slacks like flames painted on the side of some jock's sports car. Luckily though, the rain stopped around twilight, so the rest of his suit and muted paisley tie were dry. "Jackson Arthurson," he said, looking at the next flat marker buried in the earth. "Nineteen-twelve to nineteen-fifty-one."

"Horrible drunk," said the young woman, catching up to Bernard and sliding an arm around him, her tiny fingers draped into the pocket of his suit coat. She had a scent like spring wildflowers barely noticeable above the smells of rain and mud that always reminded Bernard of dead fish. "Beat his wife and kids. Caused one a serious brain injury that probably killed him, though no one could say for sure since the boy didn't die that same day."

"That's awful," said Bernard.

"Yes." She leaned her head on his bicep. It stayed there only a moment until the uneven ground they crossed bounced them back apart.

"Eleanor Lynn Ashby," said Bernard, as he absentmindedly raised a hand to brush the girl's dark bangs from her eyes. "Nineteen twenty to ... I can't make that out."

"Thief. Maid to the Danforths. She robbed them blind, let me tell you."

Bernard shrugged. "What about the Danforths? Are they here?"

She pointed to the treeline where mist oozed like a sickly river.

The cemetery followed that treeline for acres, curving in places like the various holes of a golf course. "Over that way. Several generations. You can't see them from here, but there are large family vaults."

"What about *them*?" asked Bernard. "What were they like?"

"A gambler, a whore, a murderer. Those are the big ones—the names you'd know. There are swindlers and kleptomaniacs, too, and many cousins and uncles who trod and spit on everyone they met. You don't even want to know about the kids."

"Kids, too?"

"The kids, too."

"Sounds like a rotten family," said Bernard. He felt her fingertips on the nape of his neck, a touch so light and unexpected it sent a pleasurable flutter down his spine like the onset of effects from a morphine drip after surgery. The euphoria passed quickly when her hand pulled away.

"No worse or better than most," she said. "Just richer."

Bernard stopped walking and met her gaze. Her eyes wore shrouds in the darkness, though he pictured them brown as good whiskey in the daylight. Tonight though, even the moon wore a veil, its yellow penumbra sometimes showing hints of a bowl-like form.

"It's true," she said. "Even the innocent sin. Did you really think you'd find purity *here*? Really? Of all places?"

Bernard turned and resumed his walk, getting farther and farther from the simple plot where the service had been held. The young woman hesitated just a moment, then picked up her pace and rejoined him. "I wonder," said Bernard.

"What?"

"All this talk, all this ugliness…"

"Yes?"

"Telling me all this stuff, are you trying to make me feel better?"

"No," she said. "Worse."

He nodded. *Of course*, he thought. *It's not working, though.*

The two arrived at a densely packed stretch of graves where more traditional granite or marble markers rose one foot or several above the ground. The first one they came to was black as an idol carved out of coal. "Sister Mary Agnes," said Bernard.

"A nun in a protestant graveyard. Makes you think."

"Hmmm. She died young. What was she?"

"A seducer. Your kind of girl."

Bernard didn't take the bait. He moved on, skipping several stones until he arrived at the pointed obelisk centering this cluster. "I don't see the name," he said. "Is that it? No, wait…"

The young woman separated from him, went around to the far side of the obelisk and stared at an iron plate affixed to the ground. "Beloved wife and mother," she said, not reading off the name. "That's a joke. You wouldn't believe the crimes she committed."

"I don't want to know," said Bernard.

"No, you don't. Nobody does. These are the things you won't learn from the archives of the Lone Oak Historical Society, though you might get some of the truth if you spend a few hours or maybe a week in the morgue at the *Lone Oak Weekly Times*."

"Is that how *you* know so much?"

The young woman didn't answer. The two watched each other in silence for a moment. Then the girl pointed to a stone seraph eight feet high, very feminine, with exquisitely detailed wings folded around her in a mournful embrace. "There," she said, leading Bernard to it. "That one's important. Beautiful and sad."

"What's the name?"

"You don't need the name."

"Why not? Who was she?"

"It was a *he*. You might actually find *his* story somewhere if you looked hard enough."

Bernard glanced upward at the angel's face. Traces of the evening's rain glittered on her head, with just enough moonlight to paint the trail from one droplet streaking down her cheek like a tear. "Tell me," he said. "This time, I have to know."

The young woman paused, but only for a breath. "He was a mean one. He beat her—his wife, I mean. Not every day, but often enough. There were police reports and hospitals. He used fists, belt, a broom, a bottle—God knows what else. But she outlived him. His liver was weak, or maybe it was his heart. So, when he died, she had this monument built."

"Why would she do that?"

"Maybe to watch over him. Some say she forgave him. Some say she wanted him to know she still loved him in spite of everything."

"What do *you* say?"

Another pause. "I think she just wanted everyone to remember. Whenever anyone sees that monument, this story gets told, and whoever hears it knows what a cruel bastard that man really was." Her voice crackled as she finished the tale.

He studied her. Suddenly she seemed to wear the granite angel's face, mimicking even the tear that arced along a cheek. There was still just enough radiance of moonlight peeking through cloud cover to highlight her features—the bowed head, the dark hair dangling, the hints of bare shoulders more alluring than naked breasts—though not enough to keep her scarlet dress from pretending the black of mourning.

Bernard stepped forward and took her in his arms, enfolding them around her like the granite angel's wings. He pressed her to him, feeling her warmth and chill at the same time. It had been a while since he'd held a woman so lovingly. It was an embrace born of a different passion than those he so often experienced inside him, cutting with their tiny butcher knives.

Liz. Six-three, about one-seventy. He didn't know why he chose her. She wasn't even his type: a bit tall for his taste, a bit thick in her thighs and hips, skin unnaturally tan, hair a patchwork of similar but not quite exact dyes. She was a waitress, too—another cliché in his book. He chatted her up just the same, got her number, took her out for drinks and dancing, then ... a meager few hours filled with tenderness and kisses. Only the once. Only....

Before Bernard knew the young woman had moved, she was gone. He saw her walking away from him at a fast pace. Getting himself together, he raced after her, his fine Italian leather squishing into and over the moist earth. For some reason, he felt as if he were swimming in a sea of chocolate. He even smelled a hint of hot cocoa, but that scent vanished when he caught up to the girl and grabbed her by the forearm. Then, he could smell only flowers—whatever bright fragrance she wore.

She stopped moving. "A few more stones," she told him.

"I hate these stones," he said. "They all lie."

"I know."

"Why can't they be honest?"

"And say what? *Here lies Robert Twist. Raped a girl in college and then married her to wash away the guilt.*' Or how about, *'David Lee Colquitt. Never said an honest word in his life.*' And you? What would yours say?"

Bernard didn't hesitate. "Adulterer," he said.

"Lecher?"

"Promiscuous."

"Fornicator!"

"Lover of women..."

"...women who weren't his wife."

He nodded, remembering.

He came home straight from the Courthouse that day and found her waiting, her pale, delicate hands squeezed into a fist, the panties balled up like a wad of paper headed for the trash basket. The damnedest thing was, he didn't know why he'd saved them. Nothing special about them. Just white cotton outlined and speckled with brown dots. They didn't belong to Liz. He didn't know whose they were. He couldn't even recall where he'd hidden them.

When she confronted him, she never uncurled her white-knuckled fist or let those panties fall from her grip. Nor did she brush the tear-soaked burgundy hair from her cheeks. She attacked, and Bernard denied. She swore, and he argued. She cried, and he pled. She ranted, and finally, he left.

That night, he checked into a familiar hotel. His hands quaked as he slid the electronic key card into the lock. The carpet was the color of dirt, the walls bland and paper-thin. It was a non-smoking room, but the air smelled heavily of tobacco and something else ... something sour. He let the atmosphere overwhelm him. He couldn't sleep at all. In the next room, he heard a woman crying—never the sound of a man, just her—and he imagined.... How could he not? The timing.... The horrible sense of connection....

"There they are," the young woman said, "The Suicide Family."

"Uh," said Bernard, unsure what words would fit this revelation.

"Melissa Tarquin, suicide by oven gas."

"Uh huh."

"Jerry Tarquin, handgun."

"That's..."

"Geraldine Tarquin, age nineteen, drove her car off a bridge, taking her unborn with her."

"...a little gruesome."

"Terrance Tarquin, pills. Maybe suicide, maybe not. What do you think? Was it?"

Bernard couldn't answer at first. His mind raced and circled and raced again like dogs speeding around the track. He understood that she wasn't referring only to Terrance Tarquin. Finally, he choked back the sorrowful squawks trying to escape. "Hard to say with pills, I guess. Even the Coroner couldn't answer for sure."

"Too many pills," she said. "Nerve pills. Could be suicide, could be..."

"...accidental overdose."

"Wait," she said, spinning and seeking. She pointed to a small ridge. "There."

"What?"

"Over there."

Bernard was disoriented. His mind was stuck on one thing, but the young woman had moved on to something else. "I don't understand."

"You wanted honesty. There it is. That's Hangman's Hill. Had a gallows up there a hundred years ago. Hanged seven men. Criminals. Dropped them straight into their graves."

This story felt like a release to Bernard, as if all the pain and guilt were suddenly wiped away with a damp handkerchief and a mother's gentle hand. He exhaled before he even realized he'd been holding his breath.

"No false advertising there," said the young woman.

"Still ugly," Bernard replied.

"It is," she said. "Oh, definitely."

"Still very troubling."

"Absolutely."

"Makes you wonder."

"About what?" she said.

"Well, let me ask you something. What do *you* make of all this?"

"All this ... ugliness?"

He nodded. "All these layers of bad."

"Hmmm." She locked arms with Bernard and leaned in close, shivering against him. "You know that crazy preacher down south a couple months ago? The one who predicted the Second Coming?"

"That guy who named the exact date and time, then had his parishioners give away all their worldly goods?"

"Right. Then he threw a huge party, and everybody gathered to celebrate with him and count down the minutes to the end."

"I remember. Nothing happened."

"Are you sure?"

Bernard didn't reply.

"What I think is, maybe that preacher was right all along. Maybe it was the Second Coming, and no one really noticed. Nothing changed. I think maybe nobody made the cut."

Still, Bernard didn't speak. His mind was both heavy and light. He stared off at Hangman's Hill, then lost himself in the mist that rolled along like a silvery snake. Finally, after many breaths and much silence, he raised a hand and pressed it like a kiss against the young woman's cheek. He thought he could've held it there forever.

KNOW YOUR KILLER

SOPHIA WENT THE QUICKEST. She died that first night. The killer didn't need to stalk her or make preparations. It was just a matter of showing up, then waiting for the right time to strike.

Easy.

It was as though Sophia refused to believe it could happen to her, as though she didn't take the threat seriously. She told everyone in the group that she had a date and where her new boyfriend would take her. When she got to the restaurant, she even sat with her back to the crowd. Her smooth young face reflected in the window, flaring and spectral against the moonless backdrop of night on the other side of the glass.

The killer slipped into the packed Applebee's, watching from the bar. A beer was ordered for calm and disguise. The talk all around covered classes, girls, bands, and the Monday Night Football game on several TVs with the Steelers clinging to a three point lead against the Bears. A pop song bopped and whirred from a speaker overhead—pointless and fun. The killer wanted none of that. He preferred to watch Sophia chew delicately on a saucy cheese stick.

When her boyfriend excused himself, stepping outside for a smoke, it was simple enough for the killer to creep up behind her, drop a gentle hand onto her shoulder. She didn't startle or look up, even as the blade came around the other side, drawing a candy smile across her throat. That wound looked like a professor's edit on a theme paper, and Sophia was the errant phrase that had to be marked out. The killer imagined her boyfriend returning to find her bloody and face down in a bowl of soup.

"Goddammit!" she said, finally glancing around to confront her executioner. "All right, you got me. Now get the hell out of here before Jeremy comes back and sees you."

The killer gave a slight bow and, enchanted as if in a slow dance, backed away.

• ♦ •

The serial-killer game was Brenda's idea. She said she read about it on the internet and thought it sounded interesting. She didn't use the word *fun*, just *interesting*. She brushed her dyed reddish-orange hair out of her eyes several times as she spoke—an unconscious act, parts nervousness and practicality. "I think we ought to do it," she said. "I mean, I don't know about you, but I don't want to play a fucking vampire again."

I had rejected the idea at first. It struck me as tactless and a little bit nuts. I grew up in a normal middle-class suburb and was raised by mostly-normal parents who paid their taxes, didn't drink, and went to church on holidays and the occasional Sunday. The thought of being a serial killer or a serial killer's victim seemed too much like one of my mother's irrational fears. Sure, I wasn't a saint. I smoked a joint from time to time, and I liked to escape into fantasy lands by reading Stephen King, James Patterson, Robert Heinlein, or the mandatory Tolkien. I knew how to have a good time at a party or alone with friendly college girls. But this was different, darker, off-putting. Even so, Brenda's point about vampires got me thinking. I hated the vampire game, too, and the other one—knights and princesses and stuff—had gotten stale. "What would we have to do?" I asked.

"It's pretty simple, Greg," she said. "The killer kills. The rest try to catch him and, well, you know, stay alive." She had everyone's attention now.

Ten of us were members of the Society of Creative Costumed Role-Players (everyone joked our mothers all were SoCCR moms). Brenda, Sophia, and Elaine—the blonde—made up the female members. The rest included Jason, Jackson, Larry, Kurt, Xander, and Rob, who no one knew why he joined other than that he sold coke and pills to Xander. I made it ten.

I'd been in various role-playing leagues and anachronism clubs going back all the way to when I was twelve. My favorite was a Star Wars group I joined in high school, but that ended up being less game and more cosplay, with all the girls and about half the guys just wanting to dress up like slave-girl Leia.

"How do we do it?" Someone asked. I think it was Xander.

Brenda, happy to have the floor, explained the serial-killer game to us. First, we'd separate ten playing cards from a deck: nine random numbers and the ace of spades. Whoever pulled the ace would be the killer. Everyone else would be both victim and cop, avoiding death while also trying to trap the killer and kill him (or her) first. If one of the nine took out the killer, that player would win the game. The killer, however, had to take out all nine opponents in order to be declared the champ. The killer's advantage would be that no one else knew who drew the ace of spades.

"Sounds brutal," said Jackson.

"Like an episode of *Dexter*," Larry agreed.

There were mutterings of awe. Giddy laughter came from one of the women. One of the men grumbled, "I don't know."

Ron said, "Let's get the cards. I'm ready to kill y'all. I promise I'll make it quick."

Group laughter. All of us were coming around to Brenda's idea, however twisted and dark it might have been. I remember that I thought about a passage from Kierkegaard I had read the year before in Philosophy 101 during one of those rare days when I wasn't hungover or sleeping with my head on my desk. It had something to do with how the group's sins are the one's sins, because in a group, the one can't be distinguished and therefore bears responsibility for whatever its members do. Now, we in the group were like a lynch mob, albeit in fantasy, and so all of us would suffer the guilt for any dead men hanging from a tree.

"Wait just a second," said Brenda, holding her hands palms out to quiet the rest of us. Then she brushed hair from her eyes and told us, "There's just one other rule. It has to be done off campus. Campus is base. We're all safe here." She brushed her forehead clear again—a gesture I found alluring then. "Oh, and it goes without saying, if you get killed, please please *please* shut the fuck up about who the killer is. Just because you lost, don't ruin the game for the rest of us."

———— • ♦ • ————

Ron kicked the bucket next. The killer followed him when he made a delivery, then caught him unaware as he came down the stairs at his buyer's apartment building. The rubber knife, freshly basted with red food coloring, left a dark stain from navel to sternum on Ron's forest-green pullover to show where the dope man's guts were spilling out. All he said to the assassin was, "Oh, man." Then he shook his head and continued on down the stairs.

Consensus in the group was good riddance. Most of the players seemed surprised Ron lasted as long as he did.

———— • ♦ • ————

Elaine's death caused more of a stir. She was with friends at the gay bar, where she had been dancing wildly in the glitter lights. Half-undressed and dripping with sweat, she staggered back to her table, dropped into a seat and downed the fruity cocktail that waited for her.

A few minutes later, the shooter girl in white halter and black shorts brought Elaine a rolled up scrap of paper.

"Who's it from?" Elaine asked.

The girl pointed toward the bar where the killer sat on a stool.

"You've got to be kidding." She unrolled the note and read it. It said, *You've been poisoned.* "I don't believe this. I can't even enjoy a night out with my ladies."

"Is there a problem?" the shooter girl asked. Then her eyes screwed up, and she scowled. "Oh, god," she said.

"What?"

"Are you all right?"

"What do you mean? What is it?"

"Your tongue," the girl said. "It's bright, *bright* red. It looks like you've been drinking a slushie."

❦ ❦ ❦

Brenda and I have gotten close. Every time someone dies, we comfort each other as best we can. It usually involves lots of tender kisses, while I imitate her gesture of brushing the fiery hair away from her eyes. She smiles when I do this, her face ensorcelled.

Did she come to me, or was it the other way around? It's not clear. I remember the two of us by ourselves in the meeting room at the student union. We were waiting for the crew, and we had spent about fifteen minutes discussing the brilliance of Elaine's demise. That had been more colorful a play than any of us had expected. As we talked, there was laughter mixed with a hint of tension. The next thing I knew, I had my hands on the pit of Brenda's back, and she placed hers on my shoulders, pulling me down toward her for a kiss. Her lips were chapped and hard against mine. I loved the feel of them like overly large raisins.

We stopped before the others arrived. We didn't want to, but we knew that, as it is with serial killers, privacy's the most important thing.

———— · ✦ · ————

Jackson died in a tragic mistake, shot in the head by Larry who saw him walking at the riverfront park and refused to accept it as a coincidence. Larry was the arrogant one in our group, and he would've been my first choice for a serial killer. He, like several of the others, went to the dollar store after Elaine's death and bought a little plastic rubber-dart gun. Like the killer, he dyed the darts with red food coloring. When he saw Jackson stroll the muddy track along the riverbank, he flipped out, drew his pistol and shot before Jackson knew what was happening. The impact must have sounded like a glob of hair grease splashed against a wall. It left an inky crescent riding the wave of Jackson's unibrow.

That eliminated Larry from the game as well. After his all-too-public slaying of Jackson, those of us left were forced to make a citizens' arrest. We didn't think it was right to allow someone who wasn't a serial killer to go around shooting people willy-nilly as if he were Meursault on a sun-blind beach. Larry had to be punished. We sentenced him to that worst of all prisons: reality.

———— · ✦ · ————

Well, it definitely wasn't Xander in the soup kitchen with the rope. X him off the list of suspects.

The phone in my dorm room rang. I picked myself up and staggered naked across the cold tile floor to answer. "Hello?"

It was Kurt calling with the news about Xander.

"When did it happen?"

"Late this morning or early afternoon. He was serving meals. I didn't check my e-mail until about an hour ago, so I just found out about it."

I thanked him for calling.

"Hey," he said, a bit frantic in tone, "if you happen to hear from Brenda, make sure she knows. She's not answering her cell."

"She's not?"

"No," said Kurt. "I've been trying her since I got the e-mail. She could be dead already for all I know."

"I hope not." I turned and caught a glimpse of my naked body in the mirror on my closet door. I found it kind of hypnotic the way things bended and bulged—the arc of a bicep, lens of a buttock.

"Yeah. Me, too. Who knows? She's probably off getting herself laid somewhere."

I nodded as if he could see me. "I'm sure that's it," I said. "What about Jason?"

"Don't know. I haven't seen him for days."

"Neither have I."

"Maybe he's the killer," Kurt said.

"Maybe you are, and you're directing my attention away."

"Hey, that's not funny."

"No, it's *not*. Anyway, I bet Jason got scared and locked himself in his room. He's like that. Could be waiting for the killer to finish off everybody else so it's heads-up between the two of them."

"Or maybe he *is* the killer," Kurt repeated.

"Sure," I said, nodding again. I thanked him once more and hung up before he could think of anything else to add.

So, that's where it stands. Four of us left: Kurt passed along the news that no one knew, Brenda MIA and not answering calls, me staring lovingly at my young body in the mirror, and Jason ... hiding. Any one of us would fit the profile. Or all of us.

What if there had been some trick? What if there were more than one ace of spades in the stack? Brenda brought the deck. She could've fixed it.

I shook my head. I was too close to Brenda right now to credit her with that much evil.

Even so, she could be the killer, playing me and keeping me close until she was ready to make her move. I realized that, as I'm sure she realized the same thing about me.

The odds were right. There were four of us left, which meant there was a two in four chance that either she or I drew the ace of spades. My math skills weren't great, but I was pretty sure that was a coin flip. Heads she's dead, and tails....

How would she do it? I wondered. A garrote, maybe? A hammer? It'd be too difficult to pretend to feed me to piranhas or a passel of hogs.

So, how would I do it to her? Overdose, definitely. I'd want it to go easy for her. That's how I feel about her now.

Stumbling back across the chilly floor, I climbed in under the blankets, eased beside her, spooning against her bare back. One arm slid under the groove of her neck. The other hand cupped a breast.

She jerked at the coldness of my touch. "Who was it?" she moaned.

"Kurt," I said, then told her about Xander.

Her eyelids rose. She lifted her head and twisted it to meet my gaze. There was a sternness to that look, her darkness within merged with mine. I knew what she was thinking. It was the same masterpiece of mayhem that already went through my head. There were graveyards shared between us, and blackened back alleys at midnight. We'd swallowed the same dose of *the horror, the horror*, and we were closer for it, filled with the same intense passion. We were ready to love and be loved, even though tomorrow, odds were, one of us would murder the other. Oh, and how the one would regret it—at least until it was time to start again.

WHITEBRIAR

EVERYBODY STINKS OF SWEAT and booze. My guess: there are thirty thousand people spread across the fields and around the three small stages. Thirty thousand men and women, most of them half my age and less than half my modesty. Thirty thousand folks who've spent three days loose dancing and hard drinking, with two nights in between for them to marinate in their juices, meaning they should be just about tender enough to cook.

Behind me a Frisbee flies back and forth between two groups so densely packed they appear to be lined up for a bloodthirsty game of dodgeball. To my left at short intervals are hacky sack circles where bare-chested young men in shorts and women draped in dripping tee shirts snap their feet in the air so it looks as if they're playing that improv game involving blindfolds and mousetraps.

I don't know how they have the energy. I've been here since Friday evening, and I feel exhausted despite having spent most of the time sitting on a lawn chair, getting up only for bathroom breaks or to hit one of the vendors' tents for a five-dollar bottle of water or ten-dollar slice of cold, slimy pizza.

Do I sound bitter? Don't mean to. I guess things were the same in my day. Well, not *the same* exactly. We kept our hair long, wore black clothes and pointy, feminine boots, and went to night shows where the band du jour gave us a spectacle of light, mist, and monstrous props. Shit. I feel old just thinking about it. Still, we had energy then, too.

Of course, all of us were drunk on pilfered beer and stoned out of our minds on whatever skunk dope we could lay our hands on. But these kids … wow. I've seen a thousand pill bottles already like fossilized orbs of amber holding prehistoric flies. Balloons, too, full of nitrous oxide. Plus, whatever they've been smoking, it's not all weed. I can't recognize most of the scents coming from glass or meerschaum pipes. Sometimes I've smelled apples, sometimes a rosy perfume, but more often something like burning hair.

I'm too old for festivals and rock concerts. Too settled. I work in the payroll department at a chemical plant. I wear a shirt and tie, for Christ's sake. I go to bed at the same time every night and eat the same foods at the same places. I don't partake. I'm just dull.

"You're going, man," Walt Exley told me. He waited until a couple days before so I wouldn't have time to think up an excuse. I've known Walt since high school. He got me hired on at the chemical plant back when I thought my future wife was having a baby. "Clay, you haven't been anywhere since Lindsey died. You don't have people over. I've driven by your place, and I know you sit there in the dark with your blinds drawn. You're probably slouching back in your Lazy Boy, watching the same news over and over on CNN. Well, snap the fuck out of it. It's time to have some fun."

Walt's the kind of guy who wears a hardhat for a living and repairs containers for chemicals with names so long that trying to pronounce them makes me feel like I've been poisoned. He has a short, narrow face and eyes the color of electric lemonades. He keeps a perpetual five-o'clock shadow, 1980s' Don Johnson style. His brown hair always looks ragged and half an inch too long like he keeps meaning to go to the barber, but forgets. He often passes for a much younger man. Maybe not young enough to be cool in this type of crowd, but at least he doesn't come off as someone's dad.

Me, sitting in my aluminum folding lawn chair fifty feet back from the third stage, I must look even older than I am. My face is cracked, my gut bulging beneath a blue polo shirt. I wear my ball cap with bill pointed forward to block out the sun. It's a Whitebriar cap, too—same one I bought at the concert in 1989, back when the band was another Bon Jovi, another Whitesnake, another Def Leppard.

• ♦ •

I had just turned sixteen, gotten my driver's license, and emptied my bank account of about ten years' worth of savings to buy my first car: an eight-hundred-dollar beat-up yellow Dodge with eighty thousand miles on it, no air conditioning, and a tape deck that only worked half the time.

When I heard Whitebriar would be coming to Charleston, I was overeager. I didn't have a girlfriend, but I bought two tickets just in case I could bribe myself into a date. Hell, why not? It was Whitebriar. Somebody'd go with me.

I never found it easy to talk to girls back then, and few came over to chat up the loner hanging out in a far corner of the high school cafeteria. I wore Ozzy Osbourne tee shirts and denim jackets—gray or blue. My hair, the color of wet beach sand, hung halfway down my back—not quite a mullet, but not close to the flowing curls of the average rock star. I'd been plagued with a baby face and a wisp of a mustache that looked like a stain. If that weren't enough, I wore cheap, flowery cologne to cover up the stink of cigarettes or weed I often slipped outside to smoke between classes.

When folks looked at me, they saw an outsider, a rebel. They didn't understand that even a rebel wants to fit in, if only in the rebel club itself. I tried to hang out with those who were the same kind of different as me.

People like Walt.

Walt had the heavy-metal image down pat: ripped black tee shirts, silver chains, hair rolling in natural waves down his back. His eyes stayed bloodshot from booze and blacked from scuffles. He liked to talk shit, and he knew how to take a punch. Walt also was that rare exception among our kind because he had no trouble talking to girls and so never felt the need to learn guitar or sing in a band. Walt was what the rest of us wanted to be, although our dog collars and tiger stripes couldn't get us there.

• ♦ •

Fast forward to now, Walt disappeared some time Saturday while the jam bands owned all three stages. I saw him smoking a bowl with a brunette half his age. I saw him dancing with a different woman, both of them with their hands in the air as if they were being robbed or arrested. Since then, I hadn't seen him at all.

I spent last night and most of today alone, sitting in my chair. I watched band after band perform on the third stage. I took in each show as if it were at a community theater production so that I let myself be impressed sometimes, but for the most part drifted off in a daze. These weren't my bands. I'd never heard of them: Turtle Highway, Two Brothers and a Cousin, Funk Juice, The Last Loaf. They all sounded like Grateful Dead or Dave Matthews clones.

If I'd gone over to the main stage, I might have at least recognized the headliners. I might even have heard a song or two I knew from the radio. But I didn't care about any of that. Still don't. I'm here to see Whitebriar, closing out the third stage tonight.

My plan was to take turns with Walt, one of us doing whatever while the other hung out and saved our spot. With him gone though, that fell through. Since yesterday I've had to fold up my chair, grab my backpack, and take them both with me whenever I've gone to the can.

I look at my watch, feeling even older since no one else seems to be wearing one. It's four o'clock. Two hours left before Whitebriar takes the stage. Those guys will play for about an hour and a half, giving everyone in the crowd time to mass around the main stage for the festival's big-time headliner: some Swedish pop band, from what Walt told me, that sings about swords, dragons, myths, and stuff like that.

"Well," I say to myself, "I guess another slice of pizza wouldn't hurt."

A blonde in a short, yellow-orange sundress hears me and turns to glance my way. I smile at her, and she hurries off. Her flip-flops slap the grass like wet balls of toilet paper thrown against a concrete wall. She's not interested in some middle-aged dude sitting in a chair and talking to himself. Probably thinks I'm a lunatic or a cop.

I never worked up the guts to ask anyone out for the Whitebriar show. Man, I was a timid little shit. But I'd spent the money. Twenty bucks a ticket—that was a lot back then. Not wanting to waste the cash, I gave my extra to Walt.

We went early and spent the evening downing a case of Milwaukee's Best. His dad bought it for him, saying only, "Have fun and don't get busted."

I hadn't tried Beast before, and the first sip gagged me. It tasted like somebody used a glass of lukewarm tea for an ashtray.

Walt slapped me on the back as if I were choking. "You okay, buddy?"

"Tastes like dirty bathwater," I said.

"Keep drinking. It'll get better."

He was right. By the second can, it tasted like any other beer. By the third, it didn't taste like anything at all.

When the Civic Center opened its big blue doors at seven, both of us were wasted. We staggered inside, found our seats, fell onto them, and stayed there for an hour, staring off into space. I don't even remember the opening act. It was probably Great White or Tesla—they seemed to open up for every band that came through town in the late 80s and early 90s.

I sobered up some by the intermission. I recalled stumbling up the aisle in a cattle herd of drunk teens heading for the restrooms. I remembered waiting in a long line for a spot at one of the troughs to open up. I knew I had to hold the wall while I strained to take a leak.

After that, everything's as clear to me as if it happened yesterday. We were in the fifth row, all the way on the left by the aisle. Whitebriar's giant speakers were so close they'd have crushed us if they'd fallen over. Loud, too. The sound-check roadie played one note and hammered the whammy bar on one of the guitars, and that was enough for me to feel it in my spine like I'd been impaled by a spear.

The crowd went nuts, and Walt joined in, shouting, "Woo!" and "Yeah!" as if AC/DC or Aerosmith just rocked the house and all that was left was the encore.

Not long after that, the lights went out and the fog machines kicked on.

———— • ♦ • ————

I'm standing in line for a port-a-john, my chair in one hand, my water bottle in the other, backpack slung over my left shoulder. Sunlight presses down on me like an electric blanket. My shirt's soaked through, as is the band of my cap. I hear some act jamming far away on the second stage. Can't tell who it is or what kind of music, but even from such a distance every drumbeat punches me in the ribs like a boxer trying to wear me further down.

"Come on, already," someone whines behind me. A young man's voice. Angry, frustrated, arrogant.

I turn slightly to look, but my backpack bumps the guy who must have been standing just a few inches away.

"Watch your ass, grandpa."

Really? He called me grandpa? I shake my head and face forward. All the heavy metal's long gone out of me. When I was a teenager, I'd have talked shit right back to him, taken my beating, and left content, so alone back then that sometimes even a fist to the face felt like love or a quickie on the couch. Now, I'm worn down. Alone again, sure, but I've taken all the beatings I care to in this life, even though it's life that seems to be giving me most of them.

"That's right, you old bastard. Take your rocking chair and mind your own business." I hear him laughing. He sounds like a car in the cold, sputtering as it tries to start. "Dumb son of a bitch. Why you even out here?"

"I keep asking myself the same question," I mutter.

Next thing I know, I'm shoved forward. My chair and water bottle fall to the ground. Only the sweaty back of the guy in front keeps me from going down, too.

"What'd you say to me, grandpa? Don't make me kick your wrinkled old ass."

Before I can face the guy, another man's voice says, "Now'd be a good time to shut your fuckin' hole, kid."

"What are you, his lover?"

"Kid, you might as well step out of line right now, 'cause when I get done beatin' on you, you ain't gonna need to crap no more."

I mumble an apology to the guy in front, but he doesn't acknowledge it. He's watching the show behind me. I turn to look, too, and the first thing I see is *him*—not the guy who shoved me, but the other, the one raising a wide fist that looks like a brick with graffiti painted on it: four letters, R, A, G, and E. This man's middle-aged like me, with a squared-off face and eyes so dark they seem to reflect no light. He's wearing a black Stetson, the snakeskin band around it holding a small, brown feather. His shirt and jeans are black, too, so he must be sweltering in the heat. I should pay attention to his muscular arms like crooked logs or his half-grin/ half-grimace that swears he wants a fight, but I don't. I'm stuck on the Stetson. *I know that hat*, I think. *Why do I know that hat?*

———— • ♦ • ————

When the first distorted guitar riff blasted from the megalith of speakers not ten feet away, Walt and I glanced at each other as if we were in love. I felt my eyes glaze over as the shrill notes pulsed in my spine.

There was something about a heavy metal concert in those days that left me in awe of the universe as if I'd discovered a new planet or been the first to walk on Mars. For an hour and a half, I would cease to exist outside the music, lights, and spectacle. Even the half-drunk girls in their short, black, off-the-shoulder Spandex dresses didn't excite me once a band started playing.

It was the same with the Whitebriar show. I lost myself in the dazzle and enchantment.

The band members took the stage like soldiers marching across the misty Scottish moors in some old movie. The guitarists and bass player came out first, followed by Pax, the singer. The drummer appeared behind his kit as if by magic or as if he'd been there all along. All five had long, teased hair. All five wore black eye shadow and bright lipstick. They dressed in tight pants, bulging in front, and flimsy tee shirts with some animal print or other. Only Doug Delaney, the lead guitarist, sported any kind of hat.

Pax grabbed the microphone. He offered no generic "Hello, Charleston!" to the crowd. He didn't ask "How you doing tonight?" or "You ready to have some fun?" He let out a long, trilled, eardrum-smashing wail and then launched straight into the band's latest single, "Bedroom Eyes."

Heavy guitar chords pounded in a steady rhythm like the sound of rain on a roof. Then Doug Delaney fired off his now famous pivoting-note lick.

Several thousand women screamed at once.

I barely heard Walt shout, "Fuck yeah, Clay!"

Then my right arm was in the air, fist pumping. My head rocked back and forth to the beat.

"Thanks," I say.

"No problem, dude. You can't let a motherfucker like that push you around. You'll never be safe."

"I'm not a fighter," I explain. "I'm old and worn down. Like I told that guy, I don't even know why I'm here."

"You're not as old as me," he says, "and it's obvious why you're here." He points at the faded Whitebriar ball cap stuck to my head with a paste made from sweat. "I recognize your hat. '89 tour, I think. The *Mala Prohibita* album."

"Good memory."

"Well, you know…"

"Sure," I reply, "and by the way, I recognize your hat, too."

They were drunk and stoned out of their minds. Though the music sounded tight, the musicians' bodies found no rhythm as they bounced around, head-banging and hair-whipping, trying to stay in sync with one another during the performance part of the show. Pax tripped over the microphone cord. John Doss, the bassist, nearly fell off the stage.

I didn't care. I felt consumed by the dirty sound and the burnt-strawberries scent of the fog. I was hypnotized by colorful lights and occasional jets of flame. If there existed the extreme opposite of a sensory deprivation chamber, this was it.

Whitebriar ran through a selection of songs from its first two albums, here and there throwing in tunes from the newest record. Pax howled, and Doug shredded. All five players dripped with sweat.

We in the crowd stood on our folding metal chairs, rocking our heads and trying not to fall. We swayed and held up our Bic lighters during the band's big power ballad, "Moonshine Honey." Barely-dressed high school girls raced up front to touch Pax's hand when he held it out to them. Guys formed a scrum and fought for Doug's guitar picks when he tossed them from the stage. Walt snagged one cleanly in midair as if a baseball in foul territory. We high-fived to celebrate.

Being there was so much fun. I still wonder how anyone could survive high school without rock'n'roll.

Then Doug staggered to center stage, nearly running over Pax. He ripped into a ten-minute guitar solo, loud and fast, technically amazing, but like most of these things kind of soulless. He swung his enamel-white BC Rich in a circle around his body, an instant later resuming the solo right where he left off. The spotlights on him turned from red to yellow to purple to green. Flames danced around him. Still, the guitarist's energy amped up and up until it reached its peak. Then Doug threw his guitar high up into the air....

— • ♦ • —

I introduce myself. Doug doesn't need to do the same, because I've already made it clear that I know who he is, although he looks so different now: broad and muscular where before he was lanky and thin, his black hair no longer billows out from under his hat, his face red and cracked, his neck and forearms inked in jailhouse blue. Sober, too. From a distance, I doubt I could pick him out of a lineup. Standing this close, though, I see the Doug Delaney I remember as if the one has been superimposed on the other.

We talk for a while until the line moves and I finally make it to the port-a-john. Then I wait nearby until he finishes his stint in the stink house, after which we go off to a spot as far from the bigger crowds as we can find.

Doug seems pleased to have someone close to his own age to talk to, whereas I feel as if I'm in the presence of Luke Skywalker or Captain Kirk—some childhood favorite that can't be real. That brings back all the giddiness I felt the first time I saw Whitebriar play.

He says, "I know from your hat this isn't the first show you've been to."

"I saw you guys in Charleston in '89. Again in Pittsburgh in '92, but you were already..."

"Right," he says. He doesn't need to tell me much of his story. I know a lot of it: how the booze and drugs overwhelmed him and got him kicked out of the band, how he disappeared for several years before turning up at a courthouse in Salt Lake City after beating the hell out of a cop, how he did time. But I lost track of his misadventures. I'd met Lindsey by then, and the two of us didn't pay attention to the old music anymore.

"Tell you the truth, I haven't been to a show of any kind in at least a decade. I think my wife and I went to see Roger Waters last, but it cost too much and took too much planning for both of us to get off work, find a hotel, that sort of stuff. It didn't seem worth it and really didn't have the thrill to it that it used to when I was in school." I keep rambling. Being around him makes me nervous.

"Decade, huh?" He grimaces. "Been at least that long for me, too. Checked out a couple concerts when I got out of ... yeah ... but they brought me down. I wanted to drown myself in whiskey both times. Knew I couldn't take it, though."

We hold our tongues for a bit, both of us thinking about what we've lost. Booze and music for him. For me, the only woman I ever loved. Is this middle age? To sit around talking about yesterday, sick with nostalgia, wanting desperately to regain the past like some favorite childhood toy? If so, why do people bother to leave their thirties?

...and he missed it when it came back down. It split the air between his outstretched arms and slipped through, its jagged edges of white wood crashed into his nose and chin. He dropped to the stage as if shot. The guitar made a sound like a robot's voice as it hit the ground. Then a loud hum began to build as it poured through the speakers. It grew louder and louder, becoming unbearable. Finally, the sound man killed the volume.

I try my best not to treat him like a rock star. Not that he is one anymore. Pax and the others kicked him out of the band a quarter of a century ago. I don't think he ever got back on stage. Still, he was larger than life once, and I don't want to be the guy that meets his idols, then bows down and worships. Instead, I talk about me. "I'm here with my buddy, Walt," I say. "I didn't want to come, but Walt was there back in '89, too, and he thought it'd be good for me."

"Where's Walt now?"

"Who knows? Passed out somewhere. Or maybe he found a better date. Hard to tell with him."

Doug grunts an acknowledgment. "You don't drink?" he says.

"Well, not in the way *you* don't drink. I just prefer not to, that's all."

"And you're not here chasing skirts?"

"No. I'm still ... recovering."

He gives me a funny look, urging me on.

"My wife died over the winter."

"I'm sorry," he says, because that's what people say, even ex-guitar gods.

I tell him about Lindsey: her dark red hair, her tiny frame, her fingertips that made me disappear whenever they touched my cheeks. We got together in the mid-90s, too late to enjoy a Whitebriar concert together. By then, the band had split up. This was after grunge killed the whole hair-metal genre and the names to know were less classifiable acts like Blues Traveler, Garbage, and Toad the Wet Sprocket.

At the time, Lindsey and I both worked at a cable-company phone bank with hundreds of other customer-service representatives—sitting in cubicles, taking calls from all over the country. We met by accident when she slammed a door in my face. She didn't know I was back there, but after the thump when she heard me cussing, she came back and found me cupping my eye that would be fat and purple by morning. She apologized, said, "Let me see," and lifted her hand to my cheek. Her touch felt like I'd swallowed a handful of Vicodin, stripping away the pain, leaving me numb and euphoric.

It was all over for me. I should've asked her to marry me right then. Instead, we dated for a couple years, split up twice for no good reason, and then got back together both times. At one point, she thought she was pregnant, so I needed to find a better job. Then we made our situation permanent in a small, traditional ceremony that was just a bit too Baptist for my taste.

The next fifteen years went by like a soothing breeze, a warm wind that somehow cooled on a summer day. The entire time it blew, for as long as I felt it, everything was right in my world. But it passed as suddenly as it came.

Her general practitioner called and told her that her bloodwork looked funny. He actually used the word *funny*. So, she went in for more tests, more bloodwork, CAT scans, MRIs. Pancreatic cancer, we learned. No one used the word *funny* after that.

It went downhill so fast. Before I even had time to accept the diagnosis, she was gone. She hadn't started treatment. She just collapsed one day while I was at work. I came home to find her body on the floor.

• ◆ •

The other band members had been hanging out backstage—probably drinking Jack Daniel's or doing blow—during Doug's extended solo. When the lights came up and the guitar sounds gave way to a rising murmur from the crowd, all four raced back to where Doug lay bleeding. He writhed and clutched his mouth from which several teeth had been knocked out. Pax talked to him for a minute, then helped him to his feet and tried to usher him off the stage.

The guitarist shrugged his bandmate away. He bent down, collected his shards of teeth and slid them into one of his boots. Then he picked up his BC Rich. He fixed the strap which had come loose and slid it back around him.

Pax said something to him.

Doug shook his head. He looked demonic with the blood running down his chin and his sweat-soaked black hair sticking to his eyes.

The lead singer motioned for the others to move away. He pointed to the sound man's island in the center of the crowd. Then Pax made some kind of signal with his finger. Immediately, the lights went out. A buzz of feedback whined through the speakers.

A bright white spotlight took aim at Doug. How deranged he was. He could've been the killer in a slasher film. Even so, he grabbed a fresh guitar pick and began to play as though he hadn't stopped.

All of us in the crowd lost our minds.

— • ♦ • —

I dig a hand towel from my backpack and dab at my face. It's hot enough out here that my tears will pass for sweat. The burn feels the same in the corners of my eyes.

Doug offers what sentiment he can, but there isn't much for him to say. So, either because my story has unnerved him or because my sharing of it has left him free to do the same, he opens up to me. "I know what it's like to lose everything," he tells me. "After Pax booted me from the band, I went into a spiral. I blew all my money on booze and dope. I wrecked my car and stopped paying the mortgage on my house. Lost that, too. I wrote half a dozen of the songs on our first album, so I still got a royalty check every few months, but those got smaller and smaller. I was broke, alone, soon to be homeless, and hooked on every kind of drink and drug you can name."

"What'd you do?" I asked.

"You probably read about it in the papers."

"The cop?"

"Well, yeah, later. That's where it ended up. What led to the cop was I started selling coke. I mean, I tried to get a real job, but I didn't have any experience. I couldn't find work dipping fries at McDonald's."

"I never thought of that."

"Man, being an ex-rock star's not all it's cracked up to be."

I wipe my eyes again, though the tears have stopped.

"Anyway, ended up selling coke by the gram, hanging out in dive bars and passing off the shit to anybody with the cash. One night—could've been any night, really—I sold to an undercover cop. When he tried to arrest me, I smashed his face with a bottle.

He went for his gun, but I took it from him and pistol-whipped him half to death."

I sigh. "I read about *that*," I say.

"What you didn't read is that half his buddies showed up and stomped me into a coma like they were a bunch of Hell's Angels or something."

"Jesus. A coma?"

"For about a week. I don't remember much from the fight, but when I came out of the coma, I had casts all over my body. I also had a dumbass public defender who told me everything I'd done and then worked on getting me a plea deal."

A white Frisbee lands at his feet. He waves at the people that threw it, then picks it up and flings it back at them. Without losing his place, he continues, "After that, it was prison. I was lucky. I only did two years. Or maybe I should say I got lucky that I did two years. It sobered me up. I learned to work out and keep myself in shape. I promise you, it's the best thing that could've happened to me."

"Anybody recognize you in there?"

"Hell no. Most of the cons didn't know Whitebriar from dog shit. Besides, all my hair got shaved off down to a military buzz. No one *ever* recognized me after that. Don't know how *you* did it."

"The hat," I say.

He runs his hands along the brim, stroking it as if a lover's back. "This old thing? It went with me to the pen. Stayed with my stuff in storage. It was the first thing I saw when I made it out."

"Pretty cool," I say. "So, what'd you do then?"

He grunts. "Well, spent a couple years on parole. I stayed clean and found a job working construction. I had real muscles now, so it was easier. Then I got married, same as you, but I lost my old lady to another man. I guess she found me boring. Hard to believe, ain't it?"

I shrug with my eyes.

"That's it," he says. "End of story."

"Not quite. You still haven't told me why you're here."

He stares at me in silence for a few seconds, then grins, showing off his glossy white false teeth. "One of my songs," he explains.

"One you wrote?"

"My favorite."

"Which one?"

"Riverside Jenny," he says. "It's off the first album. Wasn't one of the singles."

"I know it," I tell him, and I can hear part of the refrain in my head:

> *Early misty mornings down by the bridge*
> *Riverside Jenny takes hold of my hand....*

"We never played it live," he says. "Pax thought it was too sappy."

"You're kidding, right? You're talking about the same band that put out 'Baby, Baby, Baby' and 'Too Little True Love?'"

"I didn't write those."

"Oh."

"Pax had his own way of doing things." He strokes the brim of his hat again, perhaps finding comfort there. "Anyway, a friend of mine saw the band a couple months ago and told me they're doing my song now. I guess some pop kid did a cover of it awhile back. Now Pax probably figures he needs to play it, too." His voice trembles.

"So, who's Jenny?"

He smiles, sighs, grimaces, groans. "A girl. First real love. I was sixteen. She was younger. Everything else is in the song."

"That so?"

He nods.

"Where's she now?"

He hesitates. "She died."

"When?"

"Then."

I sigh with him and say, "I'm sorry." I know now that we're blood brothers, here for the same reasons and sharing the same pain. It's just that he's been dealing with it so much longer. I wonder if I'll still be suffering the way he is after a quarter of a century fades. I wonder if I could write a song and hide all of my sadness inside it. "How'd it happen?" I ask.

"Car wreck."

"Was it your fault?"

"God, no," he bellows. "I wasn't there. I don't think I could handle *that*. It's hard enough to deal with as it is."

Whitebriar takes the stage at six p.m. Gone are the long hair, lipstick, and tiger stripes. The band members look like five cousins doing an improvised jam at a family reunion. The high energy's missing, too. The guys stay at their stations, calmly playing their hits from the 80s. Apparently they've put out a couple of discs since reuniting at the turn of the millennium. They throw in a few songs from those, but they lack the excitement of the older stuff.

Pax stands at the microphone, wailing and screeching. His voice is still metal, even if his belly leans a little more toward soft rock. His flowing brown locks have been reduced to a tight fade. I wonder if he still feels his missing hair like a phantom limb.

Neither Doug Delaney nor his replacement rejoined the band when it got back together, and the new guitarist has a different style: slower, more soulful. I guess that's the difference between a young hotshot and a well-traveled journeyman.

Walt shows up about halfway through the set. He elbows me to let me know he's there, then mouths a few words that might be, "Having a good time?" His eyes have glazed over, his hair matted with grass and mud.

I don't ask about his day or his night. Nor do I tell him about mine. Instead, I nod and turn back to the show. It's really not that bad. Sure, Whitebriar's another has-been nostalgia act, but I need some nostalgia in my life to remind me there were good times, times when I felt happiest, times when I could move and almost float on heavy waves of rock'n'roll.

When I hear the opening riff from "Riverside Jenny," I turn to look for Doug, but he has vanished into the crowd. He's out there somewhere, glowing from one eye and crying from the other as he loses himself in the song.

His song.

My song, too, now. I'll hear it in my head for the rest of my life and remember how I've shared something powerful with someone able to understand. Love and loss, joy and sadness, the best and worst of all there is—I hear those things in the delicate melody even as it crackles when the singer loses the tune for a line or two. There's so much intensity, so much meaning. And to think, it's been there all along in a minor track the band never released for radio play.

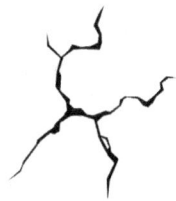

PURSUING THE FIX

THE KNOCK CAME DOWN without a whisper. It took Singer a moment to realize the door had opened an instant before the electrons in his fist would've bounced off the electrons of the wood. He stood there dumbly, a gnome-like young man with prematurely receding hair and sad eyes the color of a rolling mist after a hot summer storm.

"Oh, it's you," said a voice from the inner dark.

Singer opened his mouth to speak, but again he heard only silence. Even the noisy climbers bounding up the stairwells of his heart came to rest somewhere near the center.

"So, come in, come in. I know why you're here. No point standing there until Old Mrs. Vickers gets a hand on her binoculars and the other on the speed dial to nine-one-one."

Singer heard a muffled click, and a light awakened beyond the threshold. It brightened slowly as if someone were adjusting the flame on a kerosene lamp. Singer's eyes focused on the man in the hallway as he came into view: a tall fellow, gangly and somehow off-center like a hockey player. In a gray suit, he would've made an ideal undertaker, but the gravity was lost with his maroon Bermuda shorts and punch-bright Hawaiian shirt left unbuttoned to reveal a lean but hairy midsection. The man was barefoot also, Singer noticed as he looked down to avoid the fellow's gaze.

That was one of the problems with these deals: the embarrassment. Singer's fingers twitched as his nerves fired off the blue notes of a jazzy solo on the saxophone. His palms were sweating, and he could taste the fear on his breath despite the icy mint gum he spit out moments before stepping from his lime-green *Ford*. He should've been over his awkwardness after all the buys he'd made, all the people he'd encountered, and all the strange apartments and houses into which he'd stepped after scenes just like this one. But no ... he went into each with the same dread of rejection he felt when making eye contact with a pretty girl drinking alone at the bar.

"Close the door, would you?" said the gangly man. "You'll let all the light out. Then where would we be?"

Singer didn't stop to think about what was said. He took two steps forward and eased the door shut, reaching behind himself unconsciously to turn the latch on the deadbolt. He stood there, his face sewn with blankness, then took a few steps down the dimly lit hallway until it opened into the jaundiced glow of the living room.

This place couldn't be called spacious. A worn sofa with a Holstein print lay stretched beneath the window, squeezing sandy curtains taut against the plaster. Two recliners, one brown and one burnt orange, held strategic spots along the opposite wall. An ancient television console sat on a stand by the opening which led to another room, perhaps the kitchen. There was also a small closet door nearly barricaded by stacked milk crates harboring books, DVDs, a few stuffed yellow envelopes, and a bright pink cactus that somehow thrived in its environment. Cardboard boxes were also scattered about and a guitar case propped against a lone end table which stood out of place in the center of the room. There were no lamps, just the overhead light spitting out its dull stain. Also, Singer noticed that the place had an odor to it. At first it smelled of something dead, then of flowers, then of death again. It shifted back and forth so fast that he couldn't wrap his thoughts around it, and then he got used to it and forgot it altogether.

"Have a seat," said Singer's host. Singer hadn't noticed him standing there. "Go on, sit."

Nodding, Singer began lowering himself onto one of the recliners.

"No, not there." The man pointed a bony finger toward the couch. "Over there."

Dizzy with crimson after his mistake, Singer raised up and moved toward the cow seat, dodging boxes and an ashtray in the floor.

"Good," said the man. "Now, something to drink."

Singer stared dumbly, unsure if he were being asked a question.

"Coffee," said the man. "No, I think orange juice would be better." He stopped, stared, assessed his own judgment. "O.J. it is." He turned and disappeared through the portal.

That left Singer alone with his thoughts and uncertainties. This was the worst part: the waiting. Every second sucked at his skin like a thousand leeches. Even so, he knew he'd suffer for hours and lose every drop of blood if that was what he needed to get his fix.

His thoughts drifted, and he considered how no one would've believed this about him when he was in college making the Dean's list and working toward his M.B.A. He rarely went to bars then and never joined a fraternity. He probably met the love of his life three or four times in those years—at least, the chance existed—but he always passed her by, putting aside such things for a later, more convenient time. A sigh nearly escaped him as he looked back on those days. He choked it down, refusing to let his lips part or a sound escape.

"Here we go," said the man. He returned carrying a tall, blue-green glass of orange juice in each hand. In the dullness of the light, that liquid looked almost like honey. "Nice and cold," he said, handing a glass to Singer. "Drink up. Keep you from getting scurvy."

Singer felt unsettled accepting the glass. It didn't seem normal. Nonetheless, he couldn't risk arguing and offending his host. Best just to go along and do what he was told. Tilting the glass, he took two quick sips. It tasted sharp—at once both sweet and sour. It was as cold as if it had just been retrieved from a snowstorm. As he swallowed the first time, he felt himself stirring to life inside. Then, seeing the man staring at him, he let his head drift back and the fluid flow freely across his tongue.

"That's it. Now, isn't that so much better?"

It was. Singer had to admit the juice flared inside him like a match on its way to the kindling for a jolly campfire. He finished it off and handed back the glass, which the man took and placed on the island end table, along with his own which he hadn't touched.

"Okay, now let's see. What do you want?"

Singer opened his mouth to speak, but didn't get the chance.

"What does a man like you ever want? Bad news or good? It doesn't matter. Your birthday? Christmas? Your sister's wedding? It's always the same. The end of the world's coming. Lightning and thunder. Tornadoes. A brimstone curtain. Oh, well. You need what you need. All this talk about loving your neighbors and being kind to everyone else...? Sure, but it's still what's inside of you that's important. Am I right?"

Singer nodded.

The man didn't notice. "Got to fix *you*. Got to get *you* your fix." He paused. "Well, that's what I'm here for, I guess. I'm the mechanic."

Suddenly Singer wished he had another glass of orange juice. As quickly as the anxiety had left, it squeezed itself in again, tightening in the pit of his back, fluttering through his underarms, sweating from the ridges of his skull. How perfect everything seemed in that long-ago past when icy nectar was so plentiful. And now....

"You okay? You look flushed."

I'm fine, he started to say, but didn't.

"Maybe you should rest a minute. Lie back on the couch."

Singer wanted to protest, even as his body twisted and his legs rose up. He didn't bother to kick his shoes off. He dropped his head on the lone pillow—a small square job with a logo from some professional sports team imprinted on the front.

"That's it. Close your eyes. You'll be okay as soon as you get some rest."

The room went out of focus, and Singer realized it was his eyelids oozing shut. He tried to pry them open, but he felt as if he'd lost all control over himself.

"Go on. Close your eyes. That's it. That's good."

He did, then quickly snapped them open.

Still the man stood there, arms akimbo like some comic-book hero.

Twice more, Singer let his eyes shut. Then, twice more, he reopened them, hoping the man would leave him be.

Twice more, the man stood in the same spot.

Again, Singer's eyes closed. This time, he held them down ... waiting, waiting, waiting.

When he opened them again, Singer knew he'd slept, though he couldn't determine how long or how it could've happened. He scanned the room without moving his head.

There was the man, kneeling by the open closet door. His hands rifled through clutter, going in and out of the closet. Piles surrounded him on the floor. Perceiving the eyes focused on him, he turned slightly and said, "Oh, you're awake. Well, don't sweat it. Just hang out a little longer. I know what you need. I've got plenty. I just can't remember where it is."

Singer couldn't tell if the strange whistling sigh he heard came from him.

Meanwhile, the man kept digging things out of the closet and piling them up all around himself: a bag full of Christmas bows, a black-and-white ceramic kitten, several boxes which he opened and inspected only to quickly discard. "Hmmm," he said, his right index finger lifting up a pair of red satin panties. "Doesn't that make you wonder? What kind of decadence have you stumbled upon, my friend?" He tossed the panties aside. "Does that shock you? Does it offend the set of values you were raised to accept? Tell me a little about your upbringing. Tell me about your childhood."

Singer felt his jaw drop. It immediately righted itself, locking closed.

"Never mind. I can tell you about your childhood. Typical middle class. Not a struggle, but not a walk in the park. Your parents gave, and you took: food, clothes, toys, money, and all the guilt that pays for all those things. You went to a good school, got a good education, wasted it—you had to make your own mistakes. That's even more guilt. Screwed you up pretty good. Oh, so sorry." He paused, studying a snow globe he'd found in one of the boxes. Inside stood a polar bear in a bandit's mask pointing a pistol at two other polar bears, their arms stretched toward the sky. He shook it and then placed it ever-so-gently to the side, a tiny ball of glitter and chaos. "Don't worry," he continued. "There really are no good parents. They all screw their kids up, just in different ways: some by not loving them enough, some by loving them too much. It's easy to see what happened with yours."

Singer eased himself to a sitting position, never taking his eyes off the man.

A rubber snake slipped out of the closet, borne aloft by its tail. The man tossed it aside. "Now it seems you're torn between want and guilt and doubt and this sadness you can't begin to explain. Am I right?"

Reluctantly, Singer nodded.

"Now you're filling the holes, but what you use to fill *those* holes cuts *new* holes."

Another nod.

"Astounding, don't you think?" The man shook his head as if to contradict his own words. "Well, it's not in *there*." Leaving all the clutter and the closet door open against the far wall, the man stood, his tall, unwieldy body rising like some demonic shadow of a tree in the moonlight. "Don't worry. A little patience. I'll find it."

Another nod. Another sigh. Another nod.

"Anyway, back to your other problem. It reminds me of this ancient Buddhist teaching."

Singer felt himself growing anxious again. He didn't want to hear any more of this mumbo jumbo, this ceaseless jibber jabber. But what could he do? The man had caught Singer completely under his spell.

"It's something like this, I think. If you meet the Buddha on the road and he stands in your way, kill him."

Singer winced.

"Think about that for a moment." The man held silence for a breath, then added, "It goes on. If you meet your parents on the road and they stand in your way, kill them. And if you meet your lover on the road and she stands in your way, kill your lover."

It was too much. Singer pictured the gruesomeness of this scene. It was a hideous massacre. Blood sprayed everywhere. Singer saw himself hacking away with a gleaming silver samurai sword. Again, he winced, shaking to erase the movie that kept rewinding and replaying the same scenes.

"Oh," the man went on. His head bounced with lightness as he spoke. "I think it also says that if you meet yourself on the road and you stand in your way, you have to kill yourself."

The image made Singer retch. He started to rise as if he'd found the courage to leave. However, the man waved for him to stay seated, so he did. Still, Singer couldn't get thoughts of this vicious murder/suicide out of his brain.

"You know," the man went on as though nothing bizarre had happened, "speaking of the Buddha, think about *this* for a while. So, the Buddha sat in the shade under an ancient tree and achieved enlightenment, right? He transcended himself and transformed into a being of pure energy. That is, literally, he became light. Right?"

Singer didn't know what was expected of him, so he kept still.

"Here's the rub. E equals MC squared, right? Like Einstein said? All mass can be converted into energy if we could just figure out how, and the average guy has enough mass to explode like twenty H-bombs if we could learn to convert it. For someone as clinically obese as the Buddha, let's say thirty. Enlightening one of his thighs alone probably could level New York City. Am I right?"

This time, Singer didn't nod or sigh or stand to leave. His mind went from picturing the murder of the Buddha to imagining his detonation as if the coming of the apocalypse.

"You see what that means? When the Buddha transcended himself, he must've taken about a hundred thousand people with him. Imagine, some poor devil comes home from work, expecting a little spicy food and maybe a romp with the missus. Then, all of a sudden, someone sets off a Buddha in his neighborhood. BLAM! He achieves enlightenment entirely against his will, along with his wife, kids, friends, bosses, the taxi driver that brought him home, and the grocer on the other side of town who sold him a bag of limes just the Thursday before last. All of them—BLAM!—just like that."

This story left Singer more nervous than ever. Confused, too. His heart rate quickened, and he jumped slightly every time the man said, "BLAM!" All he wanted was to get his fix and move on. He didn't see how these stories were helping any. Plus, he'd begun to notice that the smell of the room was somewhere between rose petals and burnt toast. It was off-putting. But what could he do? If he complained about the smell or the stories or the endless delays, he might lose whatever footing he'd gained. Would the man grab him up by his sleeve and show him the door? He couldn't risk it. He needed his fix, whatever the conditions placed on the transaction. So, Singer tried his best to seem interested, but his eyes kept wandering around the room. Eventually they settled on the leaning black turret of the guitar case.

The man noticed right away. "Oh," he said, "that old thing?" He walked over to the case and knelt in front of it as if worshipping at a shrine. Stroking the shell like a lazing lover, he fumbled with latches. It opened like a silk blouse. Then he slid both hands inside and eased out the brown *Yamaha* acoustic. "This is my baby. It's my therapy." He ran through a couple riffs, bluesy and mellow but a bit off. Then, just as Singer began to dread another delay, the man told him, "I'd play you a song to cheer you up, but my baby's got a broken string. I can't make it work with only five strings."

Singer forced himself to keep a straight face, refusing to show his relief.

"*Que sera sera*," said the man. He eased the guitar back into its case and closed the lid. "Well, I think our time's about up, don't you? I guess we should get you fixed up and on your way." He rose from his crouch. His joints creaked like old stairs as he straightened his long limbs. "Yeah, *now* I remember where I put it, I think. Wait here. Don't move. I'll be back before you can say, '*Shamalamalamadingdong.*'"

Too much! Again, too much! Was that one word or five? Was it meant to be sung or muttered like a prayer for mercy? Was it some sort of code? Singer didn't use codes for anything, but he'd heard other people talk about biscuits and footballs and peaches and school buses. Whomever they spoke to always knew what those buzzwords meant. It was all too confusing and frustrating for Singer, though. It left him more dazed than hopeful. He wanted what he wanted—that's all!—and maybe he wanted too much. If so, maybe too much was just the right amount to go through in order to get it. Oh, God, but why couldn't things be simple, easy, relaxed? Why couldn't...?

He shook his head to clear the fog. He'd been so dazzled by gibberish that he hadn't realized until now that the man was gone. Singer looked around, frantic for a sign. The man's presence was a comfort to him. Now even that had disappeared. He rose from the couch, then slumped back down, equally pouting and surrendering to his own weakness and failure.

Then he stopped himself and listened. There! Sounds! Drawers opening. A door unlatching. The squawks of a medicine cabinet. The clack-clack-clack of pill bottles. He thought he heard water running, then a toilet flushed. He thought he smelled smoke. His mouth grew dry as he sucked at his tongue, and suddenly he couldn't take it anymore. He needed something to drink. Anything. Eyeballing the man's spare glass of orange juice on its island, he reached for it and drank it down with one long swallow. It wasn't icy and rejuvenating like the first glass had been. Warmed to room temperature, now it tasted overly tart, even a little bitter. All the same, it wet his lips and soothed him just enough to keep him from screaming.

He replaced the glass an instant before the man returned. A lonely orange stream ran from the corner of his mouth and dribbled onto the breast of his merlot rugby shirt. He pretended not to notice, though he absently wiped his chin with the back of his hand.

"Here we go," said the man, smiling boldly. He held out a sealed envelope.

Eager to be fixed, Singer lunged from his seat and accepted the offering. He felt around with his thumbs, squeezing and stroking. Still, he couldn't make out the contents.

"Sorry to say, it's not as much as you expected," said the man.

Singer met his gaze, saddened.

"Don't worry. It's enough to get you through until the next time."

Singer nodded. He felt relief and frustration, joy and disgust. All seven phases of grief stabbed at him simultaneously with their tiny knives. *Et tu, Anger? Et tu, Bargaining? Et tu, Acceptance?* He slid the envelope into the pocket of his jeans.

"Good," said the man. "Good. Very good. I think you've made some real progress. He stepped forward and embraced Singer before Singer knew what was happening. His bare chest felt like a warm tide through Singer's shirt. "I'm proud of you."

It was over as quickly as it began. The man stepped back, smiling and nodding. "Well, I'm sorry to say your time's up."

He placed a hand on Singer's shoulder, spun him around and marched him to the front door. "Don't worry about the cost," he said. "I'll add it to your tab. I know you're good for it."

Singer reached for the door only to find it magically open as though, shooting from the hip with gunslinger speed, the man's left hand had beaten him to the deadbolt and the knob. Bright, clear sunlight flooded the room, warming Singer's face and blinding him until he blinked twice and then could see the world again. With one last pat on his shoulder from the man, Singer stepped outside.

"I'll see you soon, my friend."

Singer didn't nod or wave. He kept walking forward.

"You'll be all right. Just keep the shadow as distant as you can."

JERICHO RILEY'S LUCK

JERICHO KNEW HE BROKE his forearm. It hurt from thumb to elbow as if someone were cutting off chunks of his skin one at a time with a pair of dull scissors. Now, as he leaned back against the officer's car, with his good hand he held the arm upright against his chest to relieve the pressure. That brought other pain. He guessed he broke a rib, too, when the seatbelt constricted. It didn't ache constantly like his arm, but every so often a fire shot through him from the center out.

The cop squatted in the road, measuring skid marks with a tape. He had said he could figure out how fast Jericho was going by using some equation that involved the length of the tire tracks and the darkness of the stain, along with maybe time travel and wormholes or whatever.

It didn't matter to Jericho. He'd been going the speed limit. Under it, really. It was the first time he had driven in ages, so he tried to be careful. He kept that from the officer, though. Jericho

Riley preferred not to see his fear of being behind the wheel mentioned in some accident report that would end up word for word in the newspaper's police blotter. It was bad enough that there'd be a story about a crazy day in which he won a car and wrecked it hours later.

His long brown right hand twitched against his chest. It sent fresh agony rocketing down the damaged arm. Without realizing it, he had clenched his fist while he considered what he won and lost.

The officer stood and circled the buck's carcass to be sure it wasn't alive and suffering. Its neck had snapped, its antlers shattered like glass. Not much blood, though. The cop nodded and walked toward Jericho. He smelled of gasoline where his hand brushed the concrete while he measured. "Okay, Mr. Riley," he said. "The ambulance is on its way. Get you to the hospital, get you patched up. I hope you can use your other hand."

"Use it good enough, I guess," said Jericho. "Haven't got much choice." He knew he could riffle poker chips with it, but not much else.

The policeman nodded. He was a lanky white fellow with a goofy overbite and a pale scar on his left side that paralleled the curvature of his chin. Jericho wondered if he had been in a bad wreck, too. That scar glowed in the gray and pink of the evening. "Good to hear," the officer said. "Now, you want to tell me again how it happened?"

———— • ♦ • ————

It wasn't like he hit the blackjack tables. Jericho didn't gamble anymore—not in eight years, not since the day his first wife divorced him, right after the bank sent its third foreclosure notice and before the credit-card companies made their threats to sue.

Just a few raffle tickets. He bought them to support the local youth-league football team. The dad of one of the players donated the vehicle—a used Toyota Corolla, candy-apple red—and the youngsters sold tickets for a dollar apiece. Jericho thought about saying no when the kid from the apartment next door came by, but he told himself it was for a good cause. He claimed twenty dollars' worth. And why not? It wasn't like Jericho had anybody to answer to, his second wife having left him for reasons all her own.

The boy, maybe twelve years old, had shined himself up in a white dress shirt and clip-on tie the color of honey. He wore black church shoes, freshly-polished, and someone had combed his hair with a flawless part on the left. If the kid were older, Jericho would've thought the boy a Latter Day Saint come to talk yada-yada with him. Instead, he told the kid, "Good luck," took his twenty ticket halves, and closed the door.

How he loved those stubs. They felt like a cross between playing cards and poker chips in his hands. He massaged them with his fingers until a thick, narcotic river oozed down his spine. He had traded his twenty-dollar cow for these magic beans. Now he grew light-headed, giddy, nostalgic for the life he used to live.

Jericho turned gambler at twenty-one. Poker, blackjack, roulette, slots—he knew and understood all the games before he tried any. Then he played on the cheap until he lost what he was prepared to lose: five years' savings he put aside while flipping burgers at a joint so small it didn't have a name. For five years,

Jericho went home with aching feet and clothes which smelled of burnt French-fry oil, only to listen to his mama complain about her hard life.

Those days were over. Jericho thanked Jesus and whoever was the patron saint of games—he believed there had to be one but, not a Catholic himself, didn't have a name for the guy.

So, Jericho set about losing. He had to lose. It was the equivalent of a college kid writing his dissertation: a lot of misery with hope on the other side.

After he burned through all five years' worth of his money, only then did he decide it was time to win. He took thirty-five dollars he earned selling plasma and headed to his hometown casino near Washington, Pennsylvania. Within two hours, he turned that money into three hundred. By the end of the night, he had almost a grand.

For years after that, he refused to go on a losing streak that was big enough to hurt him. He travelled the country, sitting in for whatever games of chance and skill he could find: five-dollar pot-limit Omaha High/Low, two-dollar slots, keno, video poker, seven-card stud with one-eyed jacks and the suicide king for wilds, and of course, no-limit Texas Hold'em—what he considered the only good thing ever to come from Texas. Jericho played hard, applying the pressure when needed, backing off when the cards died, reading his opponents, bluffing ... winning. He entered tournaments, slipped into cash games, sharked whenever he could. He loved the thrill of it, and his life was good.

His *life*.

Not his *luck*, he swore. There was no such thing as good luck. Just skill and determination.

He met Constance the year before he played in the World Series of Poker main event. He found her in Lawrence, Kansas, in the audience awaiting the start of a TV tournament. Constance Gold. Half Latina, half Jew—that interested him, being of mixed race, too. She had inky black hair and black eyes, her skin just darker than beach sand. She liked to drink kamikazes or electric lemonades while she watched the table action. She got excited whenever chips splashed the pot. If the dealer turned over an ace on the river, it left her moaning as if that were the best use she could make of a man. She didn't play, though. Didn't gamble. Didn't need to be in the middle of it all. For her, watching was enough.

They were lovers before they could say each other's names without stopping first to think. After that, Jericho took her everywhere with him. When he told her he bought a ten-thousand-dollar seat in the main event, she was as excited as he. He swore to her that if he cashed in the tournament, he'd marry her. He was a man of his word. Out of more than six thousand players, he finished in the money at number two-twenty-two.

---·♦·---

The officer wrote down Jericho's name and address. "I've got to cite you," he said, scribbling in his book. "No insurance."

"But I didn't hit anybody," said Jericho, groaning when he clenched his fist again.

"I know, but it's the law."

Looking down, Jericho saw a spot of blood on his white Bulls tee shirt. He wondered how it got there. He hadn't felt any puncture wounds. "You don't understand," he said, his dark eyes coming back to meet the officer's. "I've only had the car since, well, about three o'clock. I won it in a charity raffle. I haven't had *time* to get insurance."

The cop nodded, glanced at the wreck, then shook his head. "That's too bad for the car. Might help you, though. Get somebody to verify that to Judge Hartwick, and he might let you off. But I have to write the ticket. I'm sorry." He tore the page from his book and handed it to Jericho who winced as he accepted it.

———— • ♦ • ————

Somewhere in the house, Jericho kept a VHS copy of the ESPN episode where he busted out of the main event. He couldn't stand to watch it.

There he sat, three chairs to the right of the dealer who was a pretty, young, heavyset brunette. Jericho wore his usual plain white hoodie with hood raised—how it shone against his skin, making him look darker by contrast. He skipped the sunglasses and headphones this time.

Jericho ran with two hundred and thirty thousand chips. His opponent—a regular internet player whose name Jericho blocked from his mind years ago—counted out two-fifty. Not huge stacks at that point in the main event, but they were bigger than either player had carried to a live table.

The hole cards were dealt. The first three men folded rather than pay the blind.

When Jericho saw his hand, he forced himself not to grin or give anything away as he looked down at Big Slick suited in clubs. He raised with his ace and king, tripling the bet.

The next four players folded the action around to that young man in the big blind. He was a greasy fellow with week-old stubble from not having shaved since the start of the tournament. He talked too much, also. His mouth had put at least one player on tilt. With a casual toss of a few chips, he called Jericho's raise, probably just protecting what he already had in the pot.

The dealer flipped over the first three cards. They came up ace-ace-king, with two of them diamonds and a spade for the extra ace. Jericho had flopped an aces-over boat—almost unbeatable.

It was the young guy's turn to bet. He was out of position. Jericho expected him to tap the table and say, "Check." Instead, he grabbed all his chips with both hands and slid them toward the center. They oozed forward like a mudslide. "All in," the guy said. It was an amateur move typical of internet players who only knew how to fold or bet the works.

Jericho snap-called and turned over his made hand. "Take that dumbass," he wanted to say, but he kept it to himself.

Oohs roared down from watchers in the gallery.

The young guy showed his cards: the jack and ten of diamonds. He made his move with a drawing hand. He was four cards to a flush and holding a gut-shot straight draw to boot. None of that would've done him any good. Only one card in the whole deck could save him.

It came on the turn: the queen of diamonds.

The crowd exploded with shrieks and catcalls. Jericho thought he heard singing.

The young guy pumped his fist like he meant everything to go just the way it did. He'd dumbly sucked out a royal flush.

A royal fucking flush!

Jericho had never seen one at a live table. A couple popped up during internet tournaments, but he always figured the computer algorithms were faulty, leaving some games prone to make big hands. Never like this. Not at a real table. Not on national TV.

At first, he sat there stunned. He refused to believe it. Then he cupped his hands around his face. Those watching thought he might cry. But he wasn't hiding his eyes. Instead, he covered his lips so that no one saw the blitzkrieg of unkind words he mouthed.

Jericho rose from the table and left without shaking anyone's hand. Especially not the hand of the player who beat him. If that guy said so much as a word, Jericho would've punched him in the face.

———— • ♦ • ————

The EMT shined a pen light in Jericho's eyes. He moved it back and forth. "Did you hit your head?" he asked.

"Don't know. Don't think so."

"Any pain? Dizziness?"

"My world is spinning out of control," he said, "but only on the inside."

———— • ♦ • ————

Jericho saw that royal flush in his sleep. It was a cliff he fell off of night after night, forcing him to wake up moments before he hit the ground. It haunted him with his eyes open, too. It popped up on TV in commercials for deodorant or beer. It glared at him from billboards with ads for Gamblers Anonymous. It was like a door slammed in his face or an illness from which he couldn't recover.

The losing started with blackjack. He stayed when he should hit. He hit when he should stay. Then he dropped money playing roulette or sent it spiraling down the rat-hole of a one-armed bandit's coin slot. The first night of his honeymoon, he threw away five thousand dollars at the racetrack while Constance looked on, scowling and saying, "Isn't that enough? Shouldn't we go back to the hotel?" The worst part was that he forgot how to play poker. He misread his opponents, miscalled his hands. Anxious, jittery and sweating, he developed so many tells that he might as well have left his hole cards face up on the felt or put a sign on his forehead that said, "I'm bluffing!"

The more he lost, the more he fell into debt. He drank too much. All his money went. Then Constance, followed by the house.

Still that royal flush leered at him from its billboard. It was by the Interstate on-ramp, so he passed it every time he left home. It mocked him with its phone number and its promise of help. He didn't call until the day he saw that sign a dozen times as he drove around in a daze. Beside him on the passenger seat was a stack of papers. They detailed the Judge's final order granting Constance's request for a dissolution of marriage.

Jericho exited the hospital with his arm in a glowing yellow cast. It shone brightly resting in the navy sling tied around his neck.

It was almost midnight when the doctor released him from the E.R. Jericho had been through an MRI to confirm what he already knew: he didn't have a concussion, but two of his ribs were cracked. His chest would hurt for a couple weeks. So, the nurse shot him in the ass with a needle full of some non-narcotic painkiller. The Doc wrote him a script for something stronger, then sent him on his way with a "You'll be fine."

Jericho didn't know about *fine*, but he would survive. He always did. Of course, he'd be off work for a while. He loaded mulch at the local lawn-and-garden megastore, and he couldn't do that with one good arm.

The car bothered him. It was smashed up too much for him to repair. The buck struck the fender then bounced up onto the windshield. Startled, Jericho swerved as if it weren't too late to avoid an accident. He ended up past the shoulder with the Corolla rolled up on its right side in the mud.

Too bad. He liked that car. It was his first since Chandra—his crazy second wife—drove off in the middle of the night. She took their Mustang with her, and he somehow never got around to buying another vehicle.

Jericho shook his head to clear away memories of Chandra. He didn't want to think about ex-wives. He didn't want to think about cars. Those were of no more interest to him than the sour smells of night and the muddy fields nearby. Instead, he thought about winning. He had won the raffle, and that reminded him how it felt. A win still sent magic fingers massaging his neck like rain.

"Just luck," he muttered into the darkness. He had never believed in luck, but where were skill and determination in a raffle? Or, he admitted, where were they with that queen of diamonds? So, the queen hit, and he lost. His number came up, and he won. Pure chance.

Was it *good* luck, he wondered, that he won the raffle even though it sent him to the hospital? Was it bad luck that the buck jumped out at him at just that moment on just that road? *Is even my good luck bad?* he thought.

No. Good and bad were judgments. It was all just luck. One way or the other ... luck.

A cab pulled up to the curb in front of the hospital, its lights on and windows rolled down. The driver shouted at Jericho, "Need a ride, buddy?"

"No, thanks," he said, but changed his mind. "Wait. I think I do."

"Hop in," the cabbie told him. He was young, white, college-aged, with short brown hair and a plain face. "Where we going?"

Jericho settled onto a comfortable spot in the back. "Take me to the nearest One Stop," he said. "Or Speedway. Wherever's still open."

"Sure thing, buddy." He put the cab in gear and pulled away from the curb. "You okay back there? You look pretty messed up."

Jericho started to tell him about the car wreck, but didn't. "I'm lucky," he said. Then he said it again, testing it on his tongue.

Yes, he was lucky. Good or bad, it didn't matter. Luck was luck, and today he had a lot of it. "Let me ask you something," he said.

"Shoot."

"You follow the Powerball at all?"

"Sure," the cabbie said. "Play it every week."

"What's it up to?" Jericho asked. The answer didn't matter. He closed his eyes and leaned his head back. *I'll take the long-term payout*, he thought. *That way I won't blow it all in one day if the luck just isn't there.*

THE GOD-MAKER

THE FIRST TIME I reached *The Turning Point*, I nearly bumped into her in the doorway. She stood there tall, regal and dressed in earth tones like the queen in a kingdom of mud. Golden as a crown, her hair hung straight and short, a glittering frame for a smile so sincere and soothing it seemed as if she held a projector on her tongue that spit beams of light wherever her lips would point. The only thing off about her, in her arms she held a stuffed purple alligator—two feet long and with a grin on its face easily the equal of hers.

I met her gray-blue gaze then skipped back, embarrassed. She retreated also, held the door for me and refused to budge until she'd ushered me through into the AA clubhouse. I passed by her, crossed the smoke-filled pool hall and headed for the meeting room where I found a seat in back, away from what I thought were sharp, judgmental eyes.

That first meeting, I said nothing. I didn't so much as mutter my name when the chairman asked if there were any new members. Instead, I sat there with my head down like a schoolboy stuck in the corner for spitballs and backtalk. I'm not sure I listened at all that day, and I can't say for sure if the mud queen ever entered the room. The alligator made its appearance, however. I spotted it beside me out of the corner of my eye. Different arms held it: a man's hairy, muscular arms. I thought little about it at the time. I sat through the meeting, then stood up and skipped out before the closing prayer. I moved so quickly I forgot to get my paper signed for the judge.

• ♦ •

I arrived too early the next night, so I sat in a shadowy corner of the clubhouse, hoping no one would notice the stupid young bastard serving penance for his second DUI.

"Howdy, friend. Welcome, and keep coming back. What's your name, partner?"

"Uh...," I stammered.

"Take a breath and try again."

"Stanley Carl...."

"Whoa. First names only. I'm Righteous."

"Beg your pardon?" I said.

"That's my name: *Righteous*."

"Seriously?"

He grinned, laughed, then settled back into the grin. "Yeah, I get that a lot. No wonder I turned out to be an old *alkeeholic*. But enough about me. What's your story, son?"

"Me? I'm not.... No. Just here to get a paper signed for the judge."

"How many times?"

"Uh...." I choked on the number. "Twenty."

"Driving drunk, eh? Second time? Can tell by the number."

I lowered my head.

"Well, don't fret about it. I got here on my *first* drunk-wreck. 'Course, I's drivin' a loaded tanker at the time." More laughter. I lifted my eyes to study his affable, grandfatherly face, blow-dried silver hair, and the fringe-covered leather jacket he wore. Cheer up, son. Don't sweat it. It ain't that blue-bloody bad. You'll see."

I nodded in acknowledgment more than reply.

He talked to me for a while, made me feel comfortable. That helped me pay attention in the meeting. I still didn't introduce myself, but at least I listened. Watched, too. I studied all the faces: happy faces, harsh faces, powerfully energetic faces, the faces of businessmen and born drunks, lawyers and ladies' men, faces that could've belonged to carnies or clowns, soldiers, state senators or frustrated songwriters waiting for a break, so many faces—gray or flushed—brought low by bottles of anything, or whatever. I recognized all those faces now, though I'd never seen any of them before.

More relaxed though I was, the discussion brought my discomfort back to me. It seemed pseudo-religious and preachy. Folks spoke up from around the room, sharing their different concepts of a god they claimed had kept them sober. I shivered at times, and held back a snarl at others. I wasn't ready for any of that nonsense.

"My name's Righteous, and I'm an *alkeeholic*."

"Hello, Righteous," sang the tragic chorus.

"It's not so much about that for me," said Righteous. "This is a spiritual program. It took me a long time to get it. I denied God, then cursed God, but when I found a god I could understand, well, that's when I started to recover ... not as an *alkeeholic*, but as a human being."

I tried not to cringe while he spoke. I didn't want to hear what he was saying, but he seemed like a decent enough fellow, so I also didn't want to offend him. All the same, I rejected his spiritual mumbo jumbo and thought, *That's it? THAT is their glorious scheme to keep people sober?* I shook my head once, then caught myself and stopped, staring down at my scuffed loafers.

After the meeting, I took the side exit straight into the alley beside the club. I stumbled over a pothole the size of a salad bowl, barely regained my balance, then looked up in time to see the blonde in a flowing white dress as she handed a much younger girl what looked like one of those dancing hamsters sold in supermarkets. Not turned on, it neither danced nor sang, though it showed its community spirit by wearing a *Pittsburgh Pirates* cap and jersey.

The young girl stared at it, apparently shocked.

I heard the blonde say something, but I couldn't make out the words. Then she turned toward me as I got closer. I gave a curt nod, and she said, "God be with you."

"Yeah, uh ... you too," I muttered. Lowering my head to avoid her gaze, I marched away into the night like a toy soldier with only a single path to follow.

"**W**ho's she?" I asked, a couple nights later when I convinced myself it was time to go back. I sat in the club talking to Righteous when I spotted her entering like a wave of fog through the open door. She wore a gray dress so thin and delicate it made me think of spider webs. I studied her, searching for whatever strange toy she carried tonight, but her hands were empty. I glanced away in time to miss her stare, only to find myself caught by that of Righteous—an intimidating scowl on his lips.

"Stay away," he said. "Don't go near that'n. She's ... let's say trouble and leave it there."

"You gotta give me more to go on than *that*."

"You're young in your recovery, son. I can tell from the look in your eyes you don't even know if you're one of us yet. Even if you did, I'm not sure you'd need her crafty kind of voodoo messing with your mind." He smiled, reassuring.

I shook my head. I felt angry about his condescending attitude. "Listen, Righteous, I'm the type of guy who *needs* to know. You tell me don't talk to her but don't tell me why, and the first thing I'm gonna do is chat her up to find out the truth."

"That's the sort of thing that'll get you drunk," he said.

I shrugged.

"All right, son. I'll tell you just to keep you sober one more day."

"Deal," I said.

He hesitated, glancing around at all the pale yellow tables as if worried someone might overhear. Leaning down, he whispered, "That's Evelyn. Don't know her last initial, and don't know if she's ever said it. She's a drunk like us, and a junkie, too."

"That's why you don't like her?" I asked.

"Huh? Shee-it, no. Most of us done a little sniffin'n poppin' on the side before we got here. The day and age, son...."

"Oh," I exhaled.

"Sides, I never said I didn't like her. Hell fire, I like everybody. I said she's trouble, that's all. Especially for a pigeon like you."

"Pigeon?" I said.

"Newcomer," he told me.

"Isn't that what they call the mark in a con?"

He snarled.

"Okay, so how's she trouble?"

"I know what you're thinking there, Stanley, but it's not that." He winked at me, then paused to watch as a tall man in a striped pink shirt came through the door, scanned the room, shook his head and left. "Probably thought it was a bar. We get that sometimes." He stopped again. Scratching his chin, he said, "Anyway, there's this thing about Evelyn. The old-timers around here have another name for her. It's not very nice, but it does seem to fit."

"What is it?"

"They call her *the idol-maker*."

"Idol-maker?"

He nodded. "Yep. Even to her face."

"I know there's got to be a story behind that one," I said.

"Sure is, and it's a story that's still going on." He told me she had a few years of sobriety under her belt, and she'd really taken the program to heart. "The foundation of our fellowship is each of us finding a higher power to believe in, keep us safe and guide us. Lots of us come in believe'n in nothin' and nobody, and the *Big Book* tells us we gotta start believe'n if we want to stay off the whiskey. We don't care who you choose for a higher power, or what—even if it's a doorknob. Well, she took that idea a little too seriously and just sort of ran with it."

"How do you mean?"

He told me, "She invents gods for folks who ain't got one."

"That's absurd," I said.

"Maybe. But when you don't believe in anything, why not take a chance on something silly?"

I held out my hands, gesturing for him to stop. "Hold on, Righteous. You said she was trouble, but now you sound like you agree with her and what she's doing."

He laughed, deep and slow—sinister. "Believe? Don't know about that. But I tried her game once, and in some sick, twisted way, I think she helped me—crazy old fool that I am." Righteous told me how he'd gone to Evelyn the idol-maker for help. "She told me to give her money," he said. "Not to keep, and no particular amount. The more I gave here, she promised, the better my new god would be. So, I gave her thirty bucks I'd been keeping in my boot as a secret stash—you know, just in case I said *To heck with this, I'm gettin' good'n drunk*. In a way, that was a step in the right direction.

"Anyway, I met up with her the next night, and..." He stopped long enough to laugh. "...she gave me this ... oh, I'm embarrassed to say it. She gave me this blue and white platform boot like they wore back in them disco days. It had a fish bowl for the raised part. And..." Another laugh. "...in it was this scrawny little goldfish with white spots all over him like he'd been shot by a paintball gun. Ugly fellow. If a fish could be an *alkeeholic* like us, I swear to you, son, I'd've bet on that'n."

I shook my head, stopping him. "She gave you a disco boot with a goldfish in it?"

"Sure did."

"I'm almost afraid to ask...."

"You wanna know *why*?"

I nodded.

"That was my god," he explained. "She told me straight up, 'This is your new god. You didn't have one to believe in, but now you do. His name is Inkblot, and this is his heaven. However, he travels the universe as well. Move him from the shoe into a bowl for at least a couple hours a day.'"

"That's disturbing," I said.

"Better believe it, son. Smacked me so hard it nearly knocked me bow-legged. She told me the entire story about the great god Inkblot. Shit fire, son, I thought she'd lost her flippin' brain. But you know what? I was desperate to stay sober. Desperate as a grass-chewin' cow in a blizzard. So I took a chance and accepted Inkblot into my life."

"Ridiculous," I said.

"No, true story."

"Ridiculous," I said again.

"We have a rule around these rooms, son: never judge another man's god. I didn't have one before Inkblot came along. I took it as a joke at first, but I gave it a try. Damned if it didn't help me, too. Gave me a line on some spiritual stuff. Know what I'm saying?"

"Not a clue," I said.

He rubbed his chin and grinned. "Don't worry about it. Keep coming back. You'll get it."

I tried not to mock him with laughter, then tried harder not to scowl. "What happened, anyway? What became of your goldfish god?"

"Died."

I shook my head, no longer fighting the laugh or the scowl.

"Yeah, forgot to take him out of the shoe for a couple days."

"Sorry," I muttered, covering my mouth.

"It was crazy. I nearly got drunk over it. Came down here that night shoutin', 'God is dead! God is dead! Woe is me—the man who killed God...'"

———— • ♦ • ————

I went back to the clubhouse a dozen times over the next three weeks. I started to feel at home in that dirty brown room with its coffee-stained walls and chairs comfortable only because they were old and broken in. Before long, I knew all the faces in the photos of the AA founders, and I remembered all the banners on the wall urging *Keep It simple* and *One day at a time*. I still couldn't say I was happy to be there, but at least I'd grown comfortable.

I saw the idol-maker half a dozen times, trying not to stare. It wasn't easy, especially the evening she bent her form over the red felt of the pool table. Her body looked slender and well-defined, despite the baggy khaki cargo pants she wore. Shivering, I turned away.

Righteous met my gaze and grinned that now-familiar grin of his, free and full of life. Was that grin because I was looking at her shapely body or just because I was looking at *her*? I didn't ask, and he didn't say. Then he pulled me aside and whispered, "You know, son, on second thought maybe you *should* talk to her. If you're really one of us *alkeeholics*, maybe it'll do you some good. Know what I mean? And if you ain't one of us ... who knows? Should be fun to watch it either way."

———— • ♦ • ————

"I've seen you around."

I nodded. "Likewise."

"You always look like somebody kicked your dog today." Her tone never menaced, instead promising empathy in the tender breath sounds forming every word. She stood outside in the alley under an arc lamp, her hair cast in bright gold even under the dull yellow light. Her blue eyes pierced the night like bayonets, cutting me open as well. "Do you feel lost and lonely?"

"Sometimes," I confessed.

She didn't ask *which* times. Lifting her eyes toward the overcast sky, she said, "I take it you haven't found a higher power yet." Not giving me time to answer, she added, "You're talking to the right person ... that is, if you want one—if you want to stop feeling all alone."

I kept quiet.

She took that as a sign. "Well, you didn't swear at me. A good start."

"So, how does this work?" I said at last.

She met my gaze again, soothing and wounding me. "You give me money, and I give you a god."

"What kind of god?"

She winced.

"Okay, then how much money?"

"That's up to you. Everybody gets exactly the god they need, and it costs only what each person can afford. I take it you have money?"

"Money's no problem. I'm a lawyer."

"Good. Then let me ask you this. Do you believe in a god?"

I kept silent again.

"No?" she said, smiling and reassuring me. "Let's say three hundred."

"Dollars?" I gasped.

"You're a lawyer," she said. "You can afford it. That's just an hour's work for you. It also means you need a better god if it's to be any help. Three hundred sounds about right. So, pay up ... and you can meet me back here tomorrow at this same time."

"I...," I began. "I...," I continued. "I...." I reached for my wallet.

"Don't worry," she said. "Best money you've ever spent."

---• ♦ •---

"**How may I help you?**" The robot's red eyes fluttered, and its tiny, square head whirred from side to side. Its voice sounded like a customer-service recording from the phone company as heard through a coffee can with a hole in the end.

"What's this?" I asked.

The robot replied, "Does not register. How may I help you?"

Evelyn sat the robot down. It stood calf-high to me, took two steps forward, repeated its message, whirred and then went silent. The Idol-Maker said, "Shut down," and the robot went to sleep.

"Uhm," I said, but nothing more.

"Let me introduce you to Zao Tzu, your new god."

I laughed. I couldn't control it.

"Not a good start," said Evelyn. "Laughing at your new god? Could bring his wrath down on you. Beware of his fury."

"He's gonna smite me?"

She grinned, an electric arc in the darkened alley.

"Okay," I said after a long silence. "What am I supposed to do?"

"Wait," she told me. "First, I need to tell you about Zao Tzu. Zao Tzu was created by the universe in the same instant he created it. He was part of the infinite dust speck that became the Big Bang. In the moment he awoke to consciousness, his desire to escape caused the explosion that brought all matter into being."

"An all-powerful god made in China?" I joked, smirking.

"Oh, no," she rebutted. "Zao Tzu's not omnipotent. In fact, his powers are very limited."

"Then what good is he?"

"Whatever his limits," she replied, "he's still more powerful than you."

I wanted to keep laughing, but I didn't get the sense she was joking. I stared at the dripping honey of her hair and hid for a breath in the warm lagoons that filled her eyes. We both kept silent for a long time before I nodded in resignation.

She stretched out her hand and ran her knuckles down my cheek. Her touch felt like a soothing breeze that stroked my skin at the exact moment someone stabbed me in the back with an icicle. I felt elated and terrified like I'd just been healed and might break loose in a frenzy of tremors at any moment. I couldn't speak or move, and couldn't sing ... which, oddly, was what I suddenly felt like doing most.

Evelyn The Idol-Maker pulled away, smiled a different smile—motherly—and said, "It's very simple what you have to do. Charge Zao Tzu for an hour a day. Other than that, just pray to him for help in the morning and say thanks before you go to bed. That's all there is to it. Just don't forget to charge him up. Don't forget to plug him into the power."

———— • ♦ • ————

Over the next few months, I saw her often. I kept going to meetings long after I'd met the requirements for court, and parts of me began to buy in to the program. But *she* gave me an added reason to attend. I wanted to learn more about this new religion. I needed information, instructions, anything that could guide me along the way. The blond goddess, however, showed no interest in following up on my relationship with the god she'd made for me. She often said hello in passing, and a few times we shared a brief conversation on general this-and-that, philosophies of nothing and the moon. Rarer still, she greeted me with a smile and a hug, squeezing so tightly I wondered if we were best friends in another life. Yet there was never a mention of the robot god.

Too bad. If Evelyn had asked, I'd've told her Zao Tzu pissed me off almost every day. I'd followed her instructions, praying in the morning. "Help me, Zao Tzu," I said.

"How may I help you?" he replied.

Then, at night, I said, "Thanks for keeping me sober today."

"Does not register," he replied. "How may I help you?"

Sometimes, I answered. "I want a drink of that clear, white whiskey. Please stop me."

"Does not register. How may I help you?"

"Fix my life. It's falling apart."

"Does not register. How may I help you?"

"I'm depressed."

"Does not register. How may I help you?"

"My ex-wife's lawyer called..."

"Does not register..."

"Gaaaah! I'm pulling my hair out and wanna throw myself off a tall building."

"Does not.... Does not.... Does not...."

I kicked my god often.

He kicked me back whenever I was down: "Does not register. How may I help you?"

Without the instruction book, I never figured out exactly what Zao Tzu was designed to do. Other than ignore me in a loud, obnoxious way, the only things he seemed good at were breaking small items, walking into walls, and startling the cat with surprising frequency—I often heard a shrill cry, followed by a hiss and the sight of Wally, an orange and white blur, racing around the corner and down the hall. Immediately after the cat's disappearance, that familiar voice always chanted its irritating mantra: "Does not register. How may I help you?"

• ♦ •

"**I** want my money back!"

"I'm sorry," she said, voice warm and friendly, eyes filled with peace. "No refunds or exchanges."

My eyes, in contrast, were twin howitzers firing shells toward the sky. Not at her, of course. As furious as I was, I still couldn't direct any menace toward her. "I'm serious. I want my money back. And you can take this ... thing." I held the slightly dented robot out with both arms. "It's worthless. I want to smash that damned bastard into a thousand pieces."

She laughed as usual.

"Are you mocking me?"

"I always find it funny when people get so desperate they curse their gods."

"That's not a god," I exclaimed. "It's a Chinese robot, and not even a particularly good one." The intensity of my scowl could've disproven a thousand deities and still had enough juice left to blow away whatever devil it is that steals more souls in traffic than all the whorehouses and opium dens of the world.

Evelyn never surrendered her easy charm. She always seemed like the sky wasn't falling, even as the rest of us raced to get out of the way of the moon. "Activate," she said.

The robot whirred and squirmed in my hands. It bleated out its useless promise.

"Isn't it adorable?" said Evelyn.

"Shut down," I said. Then, to her: "It's not adorable any more than it's a god."

"Activate," she said.

"Whirr.... How may I help you?"

"Looks like both to me." She brushed a hand across the robot's forehead, accidentally stroking my arm with her small finger.

Too numb for chills or delight, I shouted, "Shut down," followed by, "You don't know what you're talking about. That *thing* is the most annoying piece of junk I've ever seen."

"Activate."

"Whirr.... How may I...?"

"Shut down. Would you please stop that?"

She giggled. Not *laughed* this time. She actually giggled like a young girl in love. It's the lone real crack I'd ever seen in her detachment.

"This is so...." I stopped dead. Those childish sounds she made disarmed me.

"Yes?" she said between short bursts.

"It's so...."

"Go on."

"Oh, never mind. Don't worry about the money. Thank you for the robot. I'd greatly appreciate it if you'd take it back now." I held it toward her again.

She accepted it lovingly, smiled and said, "What about your god? What about Zao Tzu?"

I shook my head. "That's not a god. Just a toy robot. A poorly built mechanical menace."

"How do you *know* it's not a god?" she asked.

"I just do."

"But how...?"

"Because I picture my god as something just a little bit greater than that."

She stopped giggling and blushed but kept grinning as if she'd just seen nude pictures of a clown.

"What?" I said.

"Congratulations," she replied.

"For what?"

"Looks like you're not really an atheist after all."

"I...." I stood there dumb and silent, sober yet drunk with confusion.

"Hey, Evelyn," a female voice shouted from across the room. I turned and saw a young girl in red standing over by the coffee pots. "Want some joe?" she asked.

The idol-maker replied, "Set it on the floor by your feet."

The young brunette didn't question, following the instructions she'd been given.

Evelyn also placed her parcel on the floor. "Activate," she said, and the robot came to life.

"How may I help you?"

"Cup," said Evelyn.

The robot marched in slow, steady strides across the floor, picked up the tiny white cup with amazing gentleness and ease, turned and strolled back to Evelyn. It moved without tremors or the clumsiness I'd seen from it so often. Not a single drop of coffee spilled onto the floor.

I stared on, even more dumbfounded than before. Sighing, I said, "Well I'll be damned."

Evelyn's gentle fingers brushed my shoulder. She leaned down and whispered in my ear. "Maybe," she said, "and maybe not. At least for today you've got a chance."

I'M SORRY

"**IF IT ISN'T SISTER** Mary Catherine," said the man in the whalebone suit. She knew him. She'd seen him before—his smug, rounded face, his pale lips and dark eyes, his overbearing scent of some expensive cologne as if someone had pissed on him with honeysuckle. "Good old Sister Mary Catherine," he said to his thin, younger buddy in the navy jacket and red power tie. "Always around, always scavenging alms from ashtrays."

Her name wasn't Mary Catherine—it was Helen—and she didn't have the title he gave her. She wasn't even Catholic. But she never corrected him, rarely grunted a word in his direction. She knew she had that look about her. Her dirty, worn black clothes flowed around her like a shroud, and the scarf that pinned her hair back had grown dark and dusty over time. That, along with the deep sadness in her sea-blue eyes, gave her the stereotypical look of a nun at the mission in some poor country filled with peasants and Quonset huts. Her face stayed framed in black. No one could tell from looking at her how old she was, what her former life had been like, or how many husbands and sons she'd buried. Now, as every day at this time, she sat halfway up the Courthouse steps, a plastic baggie open on her lap, picking cigarette butts from one of the many tall beige ashcans. With well-practiced fingers, she carefully pinched off the first burnt end, then the filter, separating whatever tobacco remained and adding it to her collection in the baggie. Later, she'd roll new cigarettes in newsprint, tissues, and whatever thin paper she could scrounge.

"Is she ignoring you?" said the younger man. He had a face that wasn't so much kind as, perhaps, naïve.

"Oh no, no. Sister Mary Catherine sees all. Watch those eyes. They see forever, I promise you. They're sizing you up as we speak. She just doesn't say much. Do you, Sister?"

Helen met his gaze, but said nothing, her hands on autopilot, doing their work on a half-spent Newport. She didn't dislike this man. He wasn't as heartless as he looked or as comical as he smelled. Still, she didn't have anything for him.

"Well, come on," said the younger man. "The show starts at nine and it's Judge Hartwell on stage. We better not be late." He started up the steps.

"Hold on," said the familiar one. He reached into a pocket. "Here, Sister. For the needy." He handed her some change.

She wanted to ask him for a cigarette instead, to describe for him the erotic sensations of nicotine caressing deeply tensed muscles and misfiring nerves beneath her skin. She wished to say, "A Marlboro, please, and I'll make all the miracles you want."

She didn't speak, however. She accepted his offer and thanked him with a grunt and a smile that crept up only one side of her face. Then the man and his sidekick were gone, and Helen went back to her work. She spotted more than half a Kool—a blessing, a Divine light in the world like the day her Joey Jr. was born. It lay in the tray next to the stump of a fat cigar. She shivered, not touching that foul-smelling weed, that blight, that satanic crib death of a memory.

Several men and women passed by on their way to the Courthouse. Few descended the steps at this time of the morning. Beetles in their muted grays and blues and browns crawled upward, ever upward, perhaps to be devoured by a crow. Many wore laughter like a shield as they took that first step from the street, but all were defenseless and dour by the time they reached the top. Rare were the young children, playful and belligerent, led by a mother's arm, and even they lost their joy and bluster before the hall of justice, the library of deeds, liens, warrants and grave news.

Helen watched, waited. When she'd finished her salvage, she studied the man on the far side of the steps from her. He hastily puffed on a cigarette by the next ashcan over. He was another granite pebble, no color crystals in the rock he'd made himself this morning. Like so many others, he blended with the drab background of sky. Only the cherry blossom on the tip of his cigarette stood out. After a few puffs, however, he lowered his arm and dropped the remains to the concrete, not even pretending to aim for the can.

Once the man went on his way, Helen rose and skittered to the spot. She retrieved the smoldering cigarette, hefted it to her lips and inhaled. *God is good*, she thought, for once without any sense of irony. The menthol smoke salted her lip and soothed like milk in her throat. Pleasure spread through her from a fixed point like blood spilled in a swimming pool. It calmed her and excited her and helped her forget to cry. So, she took another puff, and another after that, and then it was gone like all the other joys in her life.

Sitting down, Helen went back to work, collecting butts from this second ashcan. She rarely looked up at the Courthouse, where births and deaths were recorded, where land was transferred and people were sued or sent to prison for drinking too much and crashing their cars through a cemetery's gates. She much preferred to look down at the street where traffic passed quickly, forgotten as soon as it was seen. She could smell the exhaust, the oil, the grit and tar. It smelled like life to her, and life was gray as cars and smoke and business suits, gray as the rainy morning sky—all a blur of absence, fading as fast as it arrived.

Just as rapidly, she tore through several butts, getting barely a usable pinch from all of them combined. She scrounged through the sand, past a chunk of old, hardened bubblegum, digging for one more fix, one more piece of the paradise puzzle.

From the street below, a man came into view, walking the median between the east- and westbound lanes. Thick and hunched, he had a wreath of short hair over skin reflecting gray off the sky, the bricks and window glass. No one noticed him at first, although to see him on the median instead of a sidewalk seemed odd to Helen—that, and the square of butterscotch cardboard he held with one hand at his side.

A ghost, she thought. No one *could* see him. He was there and not there at the same time, a puff of smoke in the moonlight, a blurring of dust caught in a camera's lens. She recognized the signs. She was a ghost, too. Only a handful of folks ever saw her, and less still could describe her features even five minutes after she disappeared from sight.

Her curiosity piqued, she watched with care and a surprising enthusiasm that built to crescendo in her fluttering pulse.

The ghost man stopped directly in front of the Courthouse, almost eye to eye with Helen like a gladiator staring up to seek the grace of Caesar. He glanced once to his left and once to his right, then raised his arms, bearing up the cardboard sign that glowed like barroom neon in the gray. In bold, black letters written there with a marker were the words "I'M SORRY."

Helen blinked once to make sure there was nothing more.

"I'M SORRY," the golden sign declared.

Is there anything else? she wondered, freeing some tobacco from a golden cigarette.

As if in reply, the sign announced, "I'M SORRY."

"Look at that!" said a woman standing nearby. She had dark, curly hair and wore a red blouse framed by a black pantsuit.

The woman beside her, obviously another lawyer in navy blue and white, turned to watch through the haze of her own glimmering smoke.

Just like that, the man wasn't a ghost anymore. They saw him. All along the steps and down the sidewalks, people spun as if this phantasm would fade. Cars slowed as they passed in front or honked while driving behind. A rubbernecking driver slashed his taxi through a puddle that sent chilly water to lick the man's ankles like last trickles from a wave.

"What's he doing?" said Ms. Blue-and-white. "Is he friggin' nuts?"

Ms. Red-and-black replied, "He's apologizing."

"What the hell for? For crying out loud. Some kind of weirdo."

"Don't know."

"Think he's got a wife inside? Maybe a divorce case in family court?"

"Could be. Or maybe it's one of Judge Bannister's *special cases*."

"Ooh. Alternative sentencing?"

"Maybe."

"I wonder what he did."

"Something stupid," said Ms. Red-and-black, and that seemed to settle things. Helen wondered what they thought as they climbed higher and disappeared through a set of double doors beneath so many strange words in Latin.

For her part, Helen felt sad. Not the sad she usually felt—this was different, almost extraordinary. She scanned the area, watching folks losing interest, going back to their daily business. A passenger in a passing car flicked a lit cigarette out the window, striking the sign and spraying embers on the man's head. Still, he held his post.

What a waste, thought Helen, not sure if she meant the cigarette or the man.

"Hey, buddy," shouted the driver of another car, "why don't you...?" His voice trailed off, and Helen couldn't tell what the driver had suggested.

The man didn't move. Helen wanted some reaction from him—a blink or a nod, a raised bird and a cry of "Up yours, Pal!" Nothing happened, not even a bowing of his head in grief or remorse. The whole of his statement was on that sign.

Helen folded up her baggie full of loot and, standing, slipped it into a pocket of her black coat. She brushed dirt from her backside, straightened her clothes and marched down the steps like a sentry. She crossed the street in her usual way, without looking, and headed toward the ghost man with his apologizing letters. She stepped onto the median and stopped, her eyes a foot from his—they were blue, too, she saw now, and eternally sad like hers. She wondered what demons came to claw him at night, what cruel detectives beat him again and again in his sleep until he cried out and, as always, confessed.

The man stared back at her—a small reaction. It was enough.

Stretching a hand toward him, Helen touched her chilly, blackened fingers to his cheek, tracing a charcoal tear. "I forgive you," she said, her voice crackling.

She turned to go, but glanced over her shoulder as she went. There was movement somewhere. She felt it more than saw. One of them offered a smile. She couldn't be sure if it came from him or her. Either way, she turned her face forward again and kept going, carrying this new sensation with her as she went.

ALWAYS ONE MISTAKE

I'M ABOUT TO DIE *wearing a yellow vest*, Lonnie thought, the same idea going through his head for what seemed like hours. He couldn't feel his legs. Not even phantoms. It was as though he'd never had legs, never known a man *could* have legs. Human beings, he thought, were just torsos with mouths, all of them lumped on their backs, immobile and waiting for some Divine being to feed them or lift their heads so they might watch TV.

Cows have legs, he considered. He could see them out his peripherals: big, stinking, pasty bovine legs. One of them, broken and bloody, curved a few inches from his left cheek. He wanted to reach up and brush it away, but he couldn't free either arm from the mess of boards and shingles piled over him—the mound made heavier by the cow on top of it.

He realized there was no point worrying about it. He had other things on his mind. *Dead in a yellow vest. My brother's going to kill me.* He knew he should've taken the vest off after he finished the job. It was tacky, and it linked him to his crime. Not that anybody saw him do it. It was an abandoned house way out in the boonies. Not one car passed by at any point while he was up on that extension ladder pulling down power lines. So, he was in the clear. Probably. But he should've taken off that vest.

He didn't mind the custard-colored hard hat so much. That was the only thing saving his life. He felt it squeezing down on his forehead, tight against skin like an old pair of jeans, but still protecting him, keeping the pieces of roof from crushing his skull.

A few feet away, Lonnie knew, the girl was already dead. Tracy, she'd said her name was. Or maybe Trish. Bar whore, he'd figured as soon as he walked through the doors of the little hole-in-the-wall joint. There were only three customers: the woman, and two heavyset men in biker leather and fingerless gloves. The first thing Lonnie saw as he came in was the woman pulling one of the bikers by the arm, leading him toward a narrow bathroom door. Not much question what was going on. So, he watched her go. She dressed in jeans and a denim shirt. She had dark hair, stringy and round, that sat on her head like a wet plant. Her face was pretty in a plain way, but also kind of beaten up. Lonnie guessed she was in her early thirties, but she easily could've been twenty-five or fifty depending on whether her tight body or the deep weariness in her eyes spoke the truth.

Lonnie strutted up to the bar as if he were king of the hicks. He felt like it sometimes, but not when he wore this get-up. Maybe that's why he didn't remove the vest or hard hat—the ones he'd snatched from the back of a real maintenance truck, one that might or might not have belonged to a real electrician.

They made him feel normal—a regular guy with a regular job—and he wasn't used to that.

He had the job once. The real thing. He'd gotten his journeyman's certification while he was in the penitentiary, and when Lonnie discharged his sentence, the prison's instructor hooked him up with a master on the outside. It was a good gig, and Lonnie kept it for almost six months, before one of the customers claimed to be missing a bottle of pills from his bathroom cabinet. For once in his life, Lonnie was innocent, but the boss said he couldn't take that chance.

"What can I do you for?" the bartender said as Lonnie plopped down on a wooden stool. "We got George, Jim, Jack and Johnny. There's beer on tap. What kind? Don't bother to ask." He was a younger man with sandy blond hair dangling over his eyes.

"Dickel," Lonnie told him, "and Coke."

The barman mixed the drink, sat it down and said, "Ain't seen you in here before."

"Yeah," Lonnie grunted.

"Passing through?"

"Just doing a job." He stared down at the yellow glow of his vest. "Tell me something. This bar, I barely saw the sign. What's it called?"

"Tad's. I'm Tad." He ran the back of his hand under his nose as if scratching his upper lip.

"Okay, Tad. What caught my eye was all the rocks and shit out back. Looks like this place is growing out of the side of the hill."

Tad laughed with that cartoonish, cornball, rural West Virginia laugh Lonnie had come to know so well. It was his brother's laugh. It belonged to his father, too, and about half the guys in prison. It seemed to come from the nose like snot, except in rhythm. "Yeah, buddy. Big mudslide out there a couple years ago. Boulders, earth and gravel. Half the hillside came down around us. Swelled up on our backside and spilled around. Don't know why it didn't take the building out, but now it looks like the mountain done come to eat us up."

"Damn," said Lonnie.

"County's been trying to shut us down ever since, but nobody seems to know the right agency. So, they forget about us for a while, and I keep on keepin' on as long as I can get away with it."

Lonnie was about to ask another question, but just then the dark-haired girl came out of the restroom alone and sat down beside him at the bar. She flashed a crisp twenty and said, "Beer, Tad. I need a cold beer."

Not much of a drinker, Lonnie sipped his Dickel and Coke. It still burned going down. Booze just wasn't his thing. He'd been more into powder than liquids—at least since he was about fifteen. That's what always got him into trouble. Well, that and his brother.

As he lay there, struggling to breathe, imprisoned by wood and cow, Lonnie thought about his brother—all those arrests for break-ins and strong-armed robberies, all his dirty blue jailhouse tattoos like a litany of his crimes in poorly sketched pictures, all his lies and cheats when he kept most of their shared scores for himself so he could buy his own dope: oxycodone. Lonnie tried to recall the look of his brother grinning after their last job together, saying "I guess that wasn't such a good idea," right before the cops came through the door. The funny thing was, as Lonnie lay there, he could almost hear the sound of the policeman's Beretta smashing into Denton's skull—a squishing noise like a grape crushed beneath a boot. He could see the gusher of blood down the center of Denton's sun-reddened bald head. All the same, he just couldn't picture his brother's face—a face he hadn't seen in half a decade. Denton was off doing another two to ten, and Lonnie lacked the imagination to keep Denton's image close at hand.

The girl though, Lonnie still saw her as if she were pressing down on top of him. She had pretty gray eyes like a mountain fog, though heavier from sadness or struggle. Those were her best features, or they had been anyway. They soothed and beckoned, making it easy for Lonnie to believe she pulled lots of crisp new twenties from bikers in bathrooms.

She slipped right into conversation with him, not like she meant to pick up a trick but the way she would if she spotted a friend in a restaurant and sat down at his table. Her voice was soft and deep. It hummed on some words and trilled others like a performer bending notes on a guitar. She asked him how he was doing and why he stopped at a dump like this. She smiled at him when he shrugged or grunted a reply. She told him about driving her mother to Huntington for cancer treatments and about shows she liked to watch on television—she was a cop-drama girl. She was telling him all about her cat Bowser—"because, you know, oomp bop a meow meow," she said—when Lonnie first heard the cracking of timbers overhead. Trish-or-Tracy didn't notice. She kept talking and sipping her beer, licking the foam from her lips without realizing it.

Beer, Lonnie thought. The girl disappeared, and Denton took her place. He was thirteen—two years older than Lonnie—and already shaving. The two of them were at a neighbor's house, raking leaves for a few extra bucks. They were making slow progress because they stopped every few minutes for one to sneak a punch or push the other into the pile. The neighbor—Mr. Rance, a dark-haired salesman type in his late thirties—lay back on a maroon-and-white-striped Adirondack chair in the shade under a poorly crafted overhang of particle board he'd put up himself. Empty beer cans were scattered all around him. He had a fresh one in his hand that he stared at more than drank.

Denton looked left and right as if to make sure no one was watching. He went over to the neighbor, Lonnie following close behind. "Let me get a sip of that, Mr. Rance."

Rance nodded once and handed him the can.

Denton took a big swallow and mocked a sigh of "Ahhh."

"My turn," Lonnie said, reaching.

Denton pulled the can away, shoving his little brother with his other hand. "You're too young," he said.

"Come on. Give it."

"You're too young. Stop."

Lonnie turned to Mr. Rance, his eyes pleading as if for mercy.

The neighbor glanced at Denton, then back to Lonnie. He smiled. "Your brother says you're too young, you're too young. You should always listen to your big brother."

Something shifted in the rubble, causing more weight to press. Lonnie heard himself groan. He wondered if the cow might still be alive and moving around up there.

The thought passed and shifted to an image of Denton in jailhouse orange on the same pod with Lonnie at the Regional Jail. They were by themselves at a steel table where they played a two-man card game called Casino. They played a lot of cards while they were locked up together. People were fighting all the time in jail, and there was a bunch of yelling, cussing, threatening with shanks that might or might not exist. But nobody messed with the Sharp brothers. The Sharps took care of each other. Folks knew brothers fought dirty.

Why was he bouncing around among all these memories? Lonnie wondered. He'd heard the stories about a man seeing his whole life flash in front of his eyes right before he died. But this wasn't his *whole* life, just a few random scenes. *If you only see part of your life*, he thought, *does that mean you'll just be paralyzed? Or maybe in a coma for a while?* He tried to shake off the notion, but his head moved little inside the compressed hard hat.

For some reason, that reminded him that he never saw the fat biker come out of the john. Did that mean he was safe from cows falling through rooftops? What about the other guy with him? Or Tad the bartender? Did they get away? Or were they victims, too—more bodies for the bovine god of death?

All your fault, he heard Denton shout at him. *You and your fancy yellow. I told you to lose the costume after a job. I told you to get out of the area quick. But you had to stop for a drink, and you just couldn't help going in dressed like a clown.*

"Shut up, Denton," Lonnie muttered. He thought he could hear himself actually saying the words.

Make me, Lonnie. Loner. Loser. He thought he heard those words, too.

Maybe Denton was right. Lonnie should've changed clothes, and he screwed up by stopping for a drink. He knew that. But this wasn't his fault. He couldn't plan for everything, and certainly not for some goddamned cow coming through the roof. Then again, something always went wrong: a flat tire, a sobriety checkpoint, a neighbor watching through cracks in closed Venetian blinds. That's how it happened, how folks got caught. There was always one mistake, however small, that brought cops to the door. It's why folks went to jail. Didn't the police catch the Son of Sam killer because of parking tickets? Lonnie knew he couldn't account for every possibility. But still ... a fucking *cow*?

How'd it get up there, anyway? he wondered. Did it climb the hill and come in over the debris? That seemed the most likely. Or maybe it was up there all along. Maybe Tad kept a rooftop cow for a pet. *I'll have to ask him when I see him in hell*, he thought.

Shaking that off, he muttered, "Not dead yet." Lonnie meant to survive this. He knew the firemen would get here soon enough, though they might have to come all the way from Charleston. Where the hell was he anyway? He couldn't remember. Still, the rescue team would be here. There'd be paramedics, too: EMTs in their prissy blue uniforms. And cops.

Shit! He forgot about the cops. Out there in the parking lot in the back of his primer-gray Ford was a cache of three jobs' worth of stolen electric cables—a triple dose of unseparated copper wire. *If the cops find that*, he thought, *it's back to the pokey for me, only this time it might be in a wheelchair.*

He'd tried to play it straight. He worked a job and wanted to keep it. He was good at it, too. Lonnie could do all the calculations in his head. He knew how to trace a wire, check the amps on a socket, replace an underground line through a metal conduit.

He'd taken only a few minor shocks, and he was careful. Always careful. But some jackass misplaced his pills, or some other jackass stole them, and Lonnie found himself kicked to the curb, looking for another job without much luck. Nobody wanted to hire an ex-con for anything but dipping fries and washing dishes.

Even without a job, Lonnie put his education to good use. Or bad use. Good bad use. He knew how to switch off power at the meter so he didn't burn himself up like that dumb bastard Red Gerber at Mt. Olive who walked with a limp and still couldn't speak out of one side of his mouth where he'd been stitched back together with skin from his calves and thighs. No, Lonnie wouldn't end up like that. He shut off the juice before he started a job. He wore heavy, safe, rubber-lined gloves. He checked the sturdiness of his extension ladder before he climbed up. He also scouted the houses and farms before he went in, making sure no one lived there, not even squatters. Then, after, he waited until he had a big enough haul before he tried to cash in. Plus, he stripped all the cables down to their copper so that no one could tell where he got his load—that is, if anyone had reported it stolen yet, which he doubted.

This was Lonnie's first mistake—his first *series* of mistakes. He stopped at a bar too close to the scene of his most recent crime. He left his stash visible in the back of his truck. He wore the yellow vest and hat inside. He struck up a conversation with a girl, or she did with him. He didn't have enough sense not to sit under a cow.

He wished the woman hadn't died. She seemed nice enough. Troubled, but nice. It's not that he intended to take her into the bathroom, or else to take her home. Broke as he was, he doubted he would've so much as bought her a drink. But she'd been friendly to him. Whether it was part of her act or not, he didn't know and didn't care. She spoke to him like a human being, which didn't happen all that often these days.

"You ever been to Cleveland?" she said. "I'd like to go to Cleveland. I know it's called the mistake on the lake, but that don't matter. I'd like to see the Rock and Roll Hall of Fame. I'd like to go to a Cavaliers game. I want to stare out over the water and pretend it's a little ocean just for me. That's not bad, is it? I imagine it, and it makes me feel better."

Lonnie said something noncommittal about how it sounded like a reasonable dream. Not a pipedream. Just reasonable.

Trish-or-Tracy smiled at him, nodded, smiled again. "What about you?" she said.

"What about me?"

"What do you want more than anything else in the world?"

"To be normal," he said—words he'd never spoken to anyone. "To be normal, just for a while."

Yeah, he wished she'd made it. But she was gone, and here he lay, still breathing, somewhere between hell and the penitentiary.

Because you wore that yellow vest, he heard Denton mocking him.

That yellow vest, his brother said.

"...yellow vest." Denton's voice grew higher in pitch like a child's, or a woman's.

"That yellow...." Now it was deeper, like a blues singer's.

"Thank God he wore that yellow vest."

Lonnie's chest felt lighter, followed by the pressure on his head. He wondered if that was how the woman felt right before her spirit left her body, or if she just blinked out like a blown bulb.

A bright circle burned in his eyes. He couldn't tell where it came from—moonlight, flashlight, go-into-the-light light. It was just a painful, glaring orb that awoke as if inside him. It blinded him, stabbed at him, spoke his name in curse words. He squinted and tried to pull away, but couldn't. *A lot of watts*, he thought, and then wiggled his fingers and reached his weak hand up as if he might be able to find the off switch somewhere near a door that wasn't there.

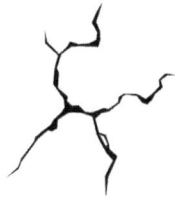

THE BURGLAR

THE PEOPLE OF KARENSVILLE, such as they are, never forget the anniversary of April 28, 1994. That was the day the burglar came to town. To be fair, he wasn't a burglar so much as a collector, but the term 'burglar' conjured up a more appropriate level of anxiety, so the townsfolk preferred that word when they thought of him.

Karensville was barely a town, hidden in the fog of the Appalachians, miles from the nearest Interstate, and with a population of around six hundred. Everyone knew everyone else, and all of them walked rather than drove to church or school. This was in the days before smart phones and unmanned aircraft. Technology had not encroached upon this tiny space. Townsfolk lived free from the clutter and stink of the outside world. They greeted one another with friendly hellos rather than mere polite ones. Mayor Boone often sat on a park bench in front of the town hall smoking a cigar that smelled vaguely of roses. Dr. Pennington sometimes saw patients on their front porch swings. Across the street from the bakery, children played hopscotch, smiling and laughing in the warm, free air of spring.

Sherman the cake-maker owned the bakery. A round man, red-faced and balding, he dabbled in delights, filling up his customers with sugary treats he learned to make in his youth when he used to travel as far as Mississippi. The cake-maker lived three blocks away in the left-hand unit of a row of gray-green townhouses. It was peaceful there, with no dogs howling in the night or heavy bass booming from the rolled-down windows of passing cars at three a.m. The noisiest thing Sherman had to deal with was the *clop-clop, clop-clop* of a horse as the police chief rode by every night at exactly ten o'clock. The cake-maker found this relaxing. It often helped him begin his nightly doze.

It was in this house to this man just after the ten o'clock trot that the burglar first appeared. How he entered remains a matter of speculation. The cake-maker believed he had locked the door and left the windows secure, but these were much less troubling times, and the possibility exists that he forgot. In any case, he lay half asleep under a sheet and light blanket, breathing in the bed smells of his own musk and listening to crickets having their nightly parley from out back, when a voice said, "Oh, excuse me. I didn't expect you to be awake." It was a soft voice, gentle and almost effeminate.

The cake-maker sat up in bed, scooting back against the headboard and holding the sheet to his lips as though he awoke from a nightmare. "Who are you?" he said.

From the shadows of the doorway stepped forward a man dressed all in black. The eye- and mouth-holes of his ski mask caught light from beyond the window and glowed like a triangle of moons. As the man drew closer, Sherman could see the outline of a large duffel slung across his shoulder and the glint of steel dangling from his hand. The stranger found a desk chair and faced it away from the bed. He straddled it, propping his arms on the back, the knife—a rather large knife with a scimitar-like curve to the blade—hanging there with the menace of distance like a spider lurking on its web in the far corner of a room. His duffel clinked and clanked as it shifted.

"Oh, let's not bother with names. Let's say you can call me Al like in that Paul Simon song. Maybe it's short for Alvin, but don't call me that."

"Why are you here? What do you want?"

"Straight to the point. I like that. Let's just say I'm what you might call a collector. A scavenger, really. I find stuff others don't know to look for. There's money to be made in just about everything."

The cake-maker shivered. He'd never been robbed before and so believed that shivering was the right thing to do. "I haven't got much," he said. "A lifetime of trinkets, a few mementos and tchotchkes. There's nothing of value here. I keep my money in the bank."

The burglar waved him off. "I don't want any of that," he explained. "I'm working for my brother. He runs a mannequin shop down south."

"A mannequin shop?"

"Yes. He makes the most wonderful mannequins, completely lifelike down to the nipples and hair. Well, except for the hands and ears. For some reason he can't seem to create a perfect hand or a perfect ear. It's sad, if you ask me. A man like him should be at the top of his game."

The cake-maker nodded as if this all made sense to him. "But what do you want from me?" he asked. "I know nothing about mannequins. I make cakes and other delicate pastries. I could bake you some marvelous and lifelike hands and ears, but they would be flower and egg. They would draw flies and melt in the heat of a shop window."

"Don't you see?" said the burglar. "It's *your* hands I want. Well, one of them. I would never importune so much as to demand them both."

"My ... hands?"

"Yes, that's right."

"Good God!"

"My brother hired me to bring back hands for his mannequins. I'm a collector. It's what I do. I see you're right-handed, so in your case, I'll only take your left."

"You can't have it!" shouted the cake-maker. "I need both hands for my work! Do you know how much artistry must go into the cakes I make?"

"A fair point," said the burglar. "All the same, I'm a collector, and collect I must. If you would please hold out your left hand, then I'll be on my way." He waved his cutter's blade in a downward swoop like a pendulum.

"No!" shouted the cake-maker, trying to hide his hands beneath the sheet.

"You wouldn't want this to get messy, would you?" said the burglar, his tone level and almost friendly.

"No, no. But wait! Can't we make some kind of deal? My hands are so important to me. I would do anything."

"Hmmm," said the burglar. "Let me think."

"Yes, think."

"I'm thinking."

"Please do."

The burglar held up a finger as if to say "One moment," or else, "Eureka!" Slowly, he reached back, unzipping his duffel and fumbling around inside to the ghostly sounds of metal striking metal at a hundred different points. "It so happens that I have this other business," he said. His hand came back holding a steel chain with thin shackle on each end. "I came across these at a surplus store in Georgia. My van's just full of leg irons."

"You ... bought them?"

"Oh, yes. Very cheap."

"You want me to...?"

"Wear them."

"Put them on?"

"And never take them off."

"That's insane," said the cake-maker.

"Perhaps, but that's the deal I'm offering. I won't take your hand as long as you're wearing my leg irons. If I come back and find you've taken them off...."

"What?"

"Well, then you've broken our deal, so both your hands are forfeit."

The cake-maker knew this was a hard price to pay. He would spend the rest of his life in chains. Yet he *needed* his hands. His work depended on them."

"Do we have a deal?" said the burglar.

"Put them on," said the cake-maker, "if this is what's required of me."

"That will be fifty dollars," said the burglar.

"You want me to pay for them, too?"

"This is my business," said the burglar. "I bought these leg irons, and I have to make a profit off them somehow."

———— ·♦· ————

The cake-maker slept little that night and, come morning, already regretted his choice. He struggled out of bed and stumbled to the bathroom where he brushed his teeth and clumsily worked his way into the shower, having to sit down on the edge and lever both feet at once into the tub. Getting dressed proved difficult as well. He couldn't slide into his boxer shorts without taking scissors to the crotch, and no pair of pants could cross the metal chain. He found a burgundy sarong in a box in the closet, shook out the dust and wrapped the terrycloth around his waist, already embarrassed at the attention this would draw.

By the time Sherman left the house, he had made up his mind to report the burglar to the local police. His silence wasn't part of the deal, he realized, and right now more than anything what he needed was someone to whom he could complain.

He found the police chief two blocks away, standing next to his horse and having a vibrant discussion with several townsfolk, all clinking and clanking with every shift of their feet. Like the cake-maker, they wore odd bottoms, open and rather indiscreet. The police chief himself, below his blue uniform top, wore what appeared to be a women's pleated skirt, perhaps his wife's. Amazed by this, Sherman paused to listen.

"...only temporary," the police chief was saying. "I'm sure this will be resolved soon enough. Until then, we do what we must."

"But my daughter can't dance," said Mrs. Carlisle, who lived on the other side of town. "She has a ballet lesson at three o'clock, and she can't even *dance*."

"She can write," said the police chief. "At least she can do that. These are the choices we have to make."

Sherman the cake-maker decided not to complain to the police chief who still had both his hands which now appeared to be rather full. "The mayor," he muttered to himself. "If the town is overrun with burglars, the mayor should be told. If anyone can deal with it, it's him."

He found Mayor Boone as usual sitting on a bench outside the town hall. The mayor was puffing frantically on his cigar with one hand and, with the other, scratching his inner thigh beneath a forest green checkered kilt.

Shaking his head, Sherman decided he might as well go to work. What could he do, after all, if the police chief and the mayor both agreed this arrangement was for the best? So, he plodded on. It's only when he reached the bakery that Sherman realized two important things: first, that he had left his keys in the pocket of his pants; and second, that today no children played hopscotch across the street.

———— • ♦ • ————

By the first week of June, life in Karensville gained a relative sense of normalcy, although there were a few changes. The police chief no longer mounted up for his nightly rounds. Despite the small size of Karensville, driving replaced walking as the preferred means of travel, so the air smelled of exhaust fumes and oil spills. The lone bar filled up most nights with lonely folks lamenting their lots as if parents mourning over their children's graves. Still, work continued, and days passed and, before long, no one mentioned the shackles anymore.

For Sherman the cake-maker, business reached an all-time high. He rushed each day to fill the many orders for tarts and cookies and towering rose-covered cakes. The townsfolk took solace in his sweets and often paid him a generous tip just for lugging his delicacies one by one to their cars. If it went on like this much longer, he thought, he'd be able to retire a wealthy man at fifty.

Such were the ideas pouring through his head that night in the first week of June when he again heard the burglar's effeminate voice from beyond the doorway of his bedroom. "Sorry to bother you like this," it said, "but I've returned." That voice sounded sad as if the burglar himself were the one wearing chains.

"What do you want?" demanded the cake-maker. "I've still got them on. I kept my word." To prove this, he pulled the covers up and kicked his legs in the air so the chains rattled like sleigh bells on a foggy Christmas morning.

The burglar stepped into Sherman's bedroom. He didn't sit, but lowered his duffel to the floor. It made no metallic sounds when it hit. "I can see that. Very good. Yes, you've kept to the bargain so far. Sad to say, I'm not here about that."

"Then what do you want?" the cake-maker shouted, aghast at his own boldness.

The burglar almost seemed to shy away from this outburst. "You see," he said, "I'm not working for my brother anymore. I have a new job. I work for an artist of some renown. Perhaps you've heard of him." He spoke a name that sounded to Sherman like some sort of Arab stew. "No? Well, he's quite famous. Publishers are clamoring for his autobiography. Oh, but when that comes out, it will be revealed that he has a rather strange quirk. He only paints with tongues."

The cake-maker let out a shriek as if he had just watched his best friend fall off the highest rung of a tall ladder.

"Yes, I know. Rather crude, but he swears they make the best brushes. So, he's asked me to collect these for him, and I am, after all, a collector."

The cake-maker caught on to what the burglar was saying. His skin turned pale and pasty in the yellow glow from an arc lamp outside his bedroom window. "You can't," he said. "It's my tongue. I need it too much."

"My employer is an artist," said the burglar. "A *true* artist. A master."

"I'm an artist, too," said the cake-maker. "Have you ever seen my wedding cakes? No one should ever get married without one of these glorious mansions in which their plastic figurines might live."

"A valid point," said the burglar.

"Every day I stir up batters and icings and sometimes jellies for the tarts. Surely you understand that I must taste them. I couldn't serve my customers inferior sweets."

"Yes, of course. That's a strong argument."

"I *need* my tongue for that."

"Indeed."

"So, you'll allow me to keep it?"

"Perhaps," said the burglar, his head nodding in the shadows.

"You have something else to sell me, perhaps?"

"Another deal?" said the burglar.

"Yes, anything," said the cake-maker.

"Well," said the burglar as he reached down to unzip his duffel, "it just so happens I recently came into a large supply of these. Don't ask me where. A disgusting place, really." He held up a large red ball with straps coming out of it. It looked to Sherman like a toy spider.

"What is that?"

"The ball goes in your mouth," the burglar explained, "and the straps latch around back."

"It's like a gag?"

"Yes, a gag. Exactly."

"And you want me to wear it?"

"All the time, except when you eat."

"If I do, you'll let me keep my tongue?"

"Of course."

The cake-maker nodded. He had to keep his tongue.

"That'll be one hundred dollars for the gag," said the burglar.

The cake-maker nodded again. It didn't occur to him that his costs were going up.

———— • ♦ • ————

The townsfolk adapted more quickly this time. The deal was that they could remove their gags only to eat. So, eating became an all-day event. Rarely could a man be seen in town without a briefcase in one hand slapping against his bare leg and a slice of pizza in the other, the red ball propped like a cold sore on his chin. All over town, the air filled with scents of grilling beef and baking bread. If this went on for long, Karensville would become the most obese city in America.

Sherman the cake-maker saw demand for his pastries rise even higher than before. He raised his prices, worked from dawn to dusk and seldom had time to think about his constant silence. He would be rich much sooner now. Rich! Perhaps he could retire at forty-five, only a couple years away, and move to Florida or farther south still to a place where the burglar couldn't find him. He refused to waste time dreaming, though. The mayor had just come through the door and was grunting and pointing frantically at a chocolate cupcake on a stick.

𝕴he burglar returned after only two weeks. Though surprised, Sherman felt less fearful and saw this more as part of the new routine. He propped the red ball on his chin and whined, "Can't you give me some peace? What is it now?"

"Eyes," said the burglar.

"My eyes?"

"Just one of yours. I have an order from a doll-maker who crafts the most lifelike toys."

"You can't have an eye," said the cake-maker, and negotiations began again.

After a reasonable time had passed for the discussion, the burglar reached into his duffel. "Well," he said, "as luck would have it, I've stumbled across a good cache of these beauties." He held up the ghostly off-white canvas of a straitjacket.

When the burglar returned two days later, he found Sherman in the living room, groaning and lying on his back amidst the shattered glass of an overturned coffee table. He reeked of excrement and blood. One cheek had crusted over from a deep gash just above his chin. When he saw the burglar, he immediately began screaming through the ball gag, but the sounds he made were more like that of a sheep discussing his religion with a hound.

"Surprised to see me?" said the burglar. "Don't tell me you thought I wouldn't return."

The cake-maker shrieked louder, rolling left and right. The shards of glass crackled beneath his numb shoulders.

"What a terrible sight," said the burglar. "You can hardly call yourself an artist anymore. Who would buy sweets from you looking like this and smelling like a broken sewer pipe?"

"Mma mma mma," cried the cake-maker.

The burglar waved his curved blade in front of him as if enjoying the feel of its movements. He played with it as if it were a paper airplane he had folded perfectly and was now ready to launch. "Well, to business," he said.

"Mma mma."

"The good news is, my brother and I are working together again. He's hired me to procure for his mannequin shop."

"Mma mma mma mma mma."

"Don't worry. We still have a deal. Your hands are safe. You have my word."

"Mma mma mma."

"It's the ears, this time. My brother needs many, many ears."

The cake-maker stopped screaming and cried instead. Through moistening eyes, Sherman saw the burglar waving his blade and realized that this time he hadn't brought the duffel bag.

UP YOURS

YOU DON'T GLANCE AT yourself in the rearview. You know what you'll see: smudged bandit eyes of troubled sleep, blond scruff not quite a beard, thick waves of blond hair not quite a mullet. The face will be older, cracked, hard—that's why you don't look, preferring to remember a younger you, when you had the same appearance but as a statement rather than a lifestyle. You wore that image well, something between a rebel biker and the portrait of a saint, tough-guy Jesus, attractive and only slightly glazed from the crack.

You're not you anymore. You feel sober, and sober feels broken, and broken feels low, humdrum, frustrated, late for work again and angry about it.

Late, pissed off, always in a hurry. You're forty-two and living with chronic road rage—which isn't a disease covered by the Americans with Disabilities Act, and won't save you from an ass-chewing at the restaurant where you fix the soups, bake rolls, and help with the dishes when they pile up.

You flash your middle finger at the woman in the blue Tesla who cuts you off, then slows.

"Up yours, lady!" you shout, your windows down, hoping she can hear you.

She appears to be too busy talking on her iPhone to notice. Can't be more than eighteen.

As you weave around her on the Boulevard, you stare her down and shout, "Get off your goddamned phone before you kill somebody."

She scowls back at you, then mouths something to the voice on the other end.

Then you're several blocks ahead of her as her hybrid putters along, losing ground. You pass one green light, then another. By the time you hit red, she's no longer visible in your mirror.

You don't really like you. Not anymore. You should have a better wardrobe, better job, better life. You've been off the rock for half a dozen years now, but does it make you feel better to say that aloud like you're one of those twelve-step crybabies? You're a middle-aged man—lonely, damaged, and abrasive.

Without signaling, a silver F-150 pulls out from a meter, forcing you to brake. You blast your horn, cursing the old guy in the truck. You shoot him the finger, and he sees you, braking too, so you think he might stop and confront you. *Do it*, you think. You haven't had a good fight in years, haven't bloodied your fists or your face for that release. But no. The man shakes his head and keeps driving, turning left at the next light.

Were you always this angry? Yes. But you thought it was just crack boiling in young blood. You never considered it might've been just you.

When you stop at the next red light, you tap the wheel with both hands in a vexed rhythm. You look right at the Kanawha River, bloated from recent rains, overflowing its banks like a busted can of biscuits. A basketball floats by, moving faster than the traffic. This amuses you, and you grin through one corner of your mouth. The water's kind of lovely: brown streaked with murky green and silver. Staring at it soothes you.

The driver behind you honks three times, the third an extended bellow, forcing you to look back up at the light. It's green, and now you're the one holding everybody up. As you ease off the brake, the other car blasts its horn again. You wave the bird as you check the rearview to see a blue and silver Crown Vic, the type that belongs to a city cop. You see his oval head, red face, buzzed hair, as clearly as if he's sitting in your back seat.

"Shit," you mumble.

At any moment, you expect to see blue lights: those flashing, melancholy strobes. You wait for it, check the mirror, wait.

Instead, the car pulls into the oncoming lane and cruises past you. You see the guy's deep blue uniform, a patch on his shoulder you can't make out as his elbow bends and his forearm rises. He extends a middle finger of his own before moving ahead, cutting into your lane and speeding away. When his lights come on, they're not for you.

You slow down, relieved, although your heart beats a marching cadence in your chest.

"That was close," you say aloud.

You've been through enough to appreciate how dangerous that situation could've become. Confrontations with police rarely go well for you. It was almost a catastrophe. Somehow, you've survived again.

———— • ♦ • ————

You've had run-ins with police. Twice, you've spent time in jail. Two cities ago, before you left Martinsburg for Morgantown to put all of I-68 and a whole wedge of Maryland between you and your past. Later you headed south to Charleston for a woman and a construction job, neither of which worked out. And you've been here since, most of this time spent sober and alone, baking bread, boiling slop, trying to stay out of trouble. You're innocent now, of everything but anger, still you shiver whenever you see a cop. You tighten up. You fight the urge to run as if you're holding a dirty crack stem in your back pocket, or someone's blood on your socks. It's a mindset you can't work your way out of. You still think of cops as the enemy, despite being no one to them here—not even a red warning light on a computer screen.

Also, of course, your mother's dead, her ashes scattered to the wind six years ago. She's often on your mind, though. God, how you've blamed her, and maybe you're right. She dealt Oxys out of her apartment, then died on you at the women's prison in Lakin, not from a shiv or vicious beating, but from a diabetic coma because she loved her soda pop too much, spending the commissary money you sent her on sugary drinks.

It's a cycle with you. You blame her, forgive her, blame yourself, then blame her more. She's an old war wound, throbbing when the weather's bad.

At least you own up to your part. Not that you could've stopped her from dealing. "Mind your goddamned business," she'd tell you. But you didn't have to intervene when the cops finally came for her—nineteen of them, guns drawn, ready to put her down if she spit. She was caught, her life in the lawyers' hands now. You could've kept your head down.

You were cracked out and crazy in the living room when they took her. You heard the cops threaten. You heard your mama cussing, "Motherfuckers! You goddamned sons of whores!" If you'd just done what she said and minded your business, you'd have kept a clean record. Instead, you ran outside where you saw blue lights staining her lined, sallow face while she cried and cursed on the ground. You leapt down the porch stairs, yelling, "You hurt her, I'll fucking kill you," right before two officers hit you with their Tasers and you dropped like a broken tree limb to the lawn.

The Martinsburg prosecutor charged you with misdemeanor Obstruction and felony Terroristic Threats. The worst charge was later dropped. Still, you spent three months at Eastern Regional Jail, unable to make the fifty-thousand-dollar bond. When your public defender eventually worked out a plea deal, dropping your charges down to just the misdemeanor, you'd been locked up long enough that the judge sentenced you to time served.

Three months. Not so long. You only smoked rock once on the inside.

$\mathfrak{Y}$ou're late, of course. The day manager says your name when you walk in, nothing else. He doesn't scold you as expected. You think he's a little afraid of you, though you've never said a vicious word to him. He's a skinny guy, at least fifteen years your junior. He has hair the color of yours and eyes the same river-mist gray. Add some muscles and scruff, he could be you at that age. Dresses better, though, in white button-ups. He's openly gay, and you wonder if you scare him because he thinks you're a hick and maybe bigoted. But he doesn't know you—that you wouldn't judge anybody for anything, not after all you've done in the days when filling your pipe was all that mattered.

Do you ever attempt to rest his mind? No. You know that mystery can be a sort of power. Having power over your boss makes life easier.

"Apron," you say.

He reaches into a plastic-wrapped bundle fresh from the cleaner. Hands you one right off the top. "Vegetable-beef today," he says.

You grunt your acknowledgment. Vegetable-beef soup means yesterday's leftovers stewed in a massive pot, stirred all morning to keep from settling. Not many spices added, other than a bit of cayenne pepper. That's something you learned in jail: no matter what you're told on kitchen duty, always add cayenne pepper to the shitty food.

"Opening soon for lunch," he says. "Better get to it."

You grunt. A man of few words. You learned that in jail, too.

Your second time was after all the bottles of Pepsi and Coca Cola killed your mom. Or after she committed suicide by soda pop. She was still your mother, no matter what crazy shit she did. She suffered from her own drug problem—different from yours, but the same in what she'd do to support it. She chased pills. She dealt pills. She loved pills. And you loved her. When she was forty and still getting in fistfights outside of local bars, you loved her. When she stupidly sold to snitches and cops until you both ended up in the clink, you loved her. So, when you found out she had *the sugar*, as she called it, you still sent her money, despite knowing she'd spend it on sweets, having traded one addiction for another.

You mourned by relapsing for the first time in months, wandering blind through a six-week bender. Most of that time is lost to you. You don't recall the punched windows that scarred your fists, the bricks that scraped your face, the broken beer bottle you waved like a sword, threatening some old couple on the streets for no coherent reason. The couple testified that you didn't ask for money, but they gave it to you anyway. Seventeen dollars. Enough to make the Aggravated Robbery charge against you stick, if the prosecutor and judge wanted it to. But you loved your mother, and her recent death brought you mercy.

You spent a year in drug court to get the charge dismissed. You went to those godawful NA meetings, picked up trash on the side of thirty roads, and earned your walking papers, along with a stern warning not to fuck up in Martinsburg again.

Lunchtime comes, and you're hungry. You can eat the soup and rolls for free, along with a discount on whatever the house special is, but you don't want anything to do with that. You wish you'd never have to see vegetable-beef soup again. It smells like sewage in your mind. You'd rather eat sewage, eat it with a fork. The rolls are okay. You'll often sneak one or two when no one's looking. The warm scent of baking bread is what you imagine paradise smells like and, since this is the closest you'll come to any kind of heaven, you breathe it in.

But you need a meal with substance. On your lunchbreak, you cut out for a quick trip across the river to the nearest hot deli. A steak sub sounds like a winner, and you're picturing it when you pull onto the parking lot. You're not angry at the moment, and there's a favorite song on the radio to which your stomach growls in rhythm. You're so distracted you don't notice the six silver cars and SUVs filling up one side of the lot. If you'd seen them, you'd have turned around, wouldn't you? You haven't seen that many police vehicles in a cluster since the time your mom got thrown to the ground and you were Tasered. That many cop cars should come with a trigger warning. Then again, that many *is* a sort of trigger warning, but you've missed it—your mind on the past, the song on the radio, your hunger, the brown-bread scent of heaven.

When the song ends you climb from your Chevy and enter the restaurant, stopping cold, paralyzed by the stuff of nightmares. Seven policemen are lined up in front of you, two or three others already seated nearby with their red trays of sandwiches and fries. From behind, you can't tell them apart except for the color of stubble on their round, pink heads—like racing stripes on minivans. There are a couple of dirty-blonds and a ginger. The rest are capped in a menacing five-o'clock shadow as if their necks are upside down. An army of clones. Seven cops. Seven of the enemy standing right in front of you, and you don't know if it freaks you out more that the line's so long or that one of those bull-necked thugs might be the guy you traded middle fingers with in this morning's rush-hour traffic.

Your instinct tells you to flee but your brain intervenes, more rational these days. Leaving now would be the most suspicious thing you could do, guaranteed to draw attention. So you step up behind the last in line and stand with your hands in your pockets, fumbling with keys and loose dollar bills.

You've never been this close to a cop before without tickets, handcuffs, Tasers, or stomping involved. You haven't studied their midnight blue uniforms that look like they're made of heavy sandpaper. Can't be comfortable. The neck of the guy in front of you sweats beads that seem to run upward, defying gravity. Looking along the line, you see it's the same with all of these men. They must be miserable, you think, and just like that, you pity them. Why not? They're not the ones that threw your mama to the ground.

What's taking so long? you wonder.

Leaning slightly right for a better view, you see the officer up front trying to foist a coupon on the tattooed teen behind the register. The kid has glassy eyes and an expression that resembles yours: anxious, uncertain, worried. He fumbles with the coupon, unable to get it to scan. He doesn't seem to know what to do next. The coupon slips through his hands. He struggles with picking it up, finally pushes it in front of the laser. You hear the digital beep of the barcode being accepted.

The cop orders—you don't hear what. He receives his tray and slides down the counter.

"Your drink," the cashier says, already turning toward a soda machine which spews a stream of Dr. Pepper. He hands the cup over, then turns to the next cop in the queue. "What can I get cooking for you?"

The next cop steps up, his right arm rising as if he's drawing his weapon. You flinch before you see the small rectangle of white paper in his hand.

"Jesus H. Christ," you mutter, hoping no one heard you.

You're on guard now, not out of fear so much as frustration. You glance down along the row of cops and see the same clipping in every hand. The cashier—who looks prepubescent to you now—has begun his next battle with paper, barcode, laser. Finishing your thought under your breath, you add, "...on a motherfucking crutch."

Your mother wasn't a bad mother. A criminal, sure, and prone to her desires. But she treated you well enough, loved you, never screwed up Christmas, knew how to cook. And you weren't a bad son. Lazy maybe, and a bit shiftless. You leeched off her, but you never stole from her. When those Martinsburg pigs put her on the ground, you tried to defend her. You suffered for her as much as she suffered for you.

So, why do you feel guilty? Some things never seem to go away.

———— • ♦ • ————

"Hey, you," one of the cops says from off to your left. You make out the hulking blue shape in your peripheral. "Buddy. You in the apron."

You look down, embarrassed to realize you're still wearing your freshly-stained apron from work.

"Hey, buddy," the officer says.

If you face him, you're certain there's a mean stare waiting in his squinted eyes. He's judging you, studying your nervousness. You're sure of it.

He advances.

You swivel to meet his gaze. It's a slow turn, tense, like in a Clint Eastwood movie. It's all in your head. These guys don't know you. They can't. Not unless...

He's two feet away from you now, looming like a drill sergeant.

Does he recognize you? Is he the one you flipped off this morning? The one who sent you the bird in turn? It's so hard to tell one of these men from another.

The officer says, "We got an extra. You want it?" He offers you a rectangle of paper. "Hate to see it go to waste." He claps you on the shoulder with one hand while waving the little coupon in the other.

You hold out your hand timidly in a sort of automated motion. It's as if you've been pulled over for drunken driving. Now you have to walk the line. Now you have to touch your nose. Now you have to count backward from a hundred.

"Thanks," you say, your voice a croak.

"Sure thing, buddy. Two dollars off. Today only. Can't beat that."

"Thanks," you say again, and unable to find an angle of reproach, you repeat it once more.

The cop pats your shoulder and turns away. You're left holding your arm in the air as if just freed from his cuffs, unsure what to do with your release.

———— • ♦ • ————

The last time you visited your mother at Lakin Correctional Center, she looked healthy, well, clean. Her hair had grayed but her skin appeared smoother, her expression lightened as if unburdened of the horrors she ingested over the years. She seemed happier, too, as though prison was what she'd been missing all her life.

You kept clean for a while, also—took a job with a Martinsburg contractor, worked your ass off to send her money every month. Came home sunburned and sweaty every night. You earned, and she was thriving in her new environment. Sure, it wasn't hard to figure out what she spent the money on: soda pop and contraband cigarettes. It didn't matter. Not to you. The woman had her habits, but at least they made her happy. You wouldn't rob her of that.

Who'd have believed she'd survive years of opiates, tobacco and booze, only for sugar to hold the headsman's ax? Looking back, you're okay with it. Sometimes you raise a cup of cold pop, as if in toast to stronger spirits, or as if she might bless you for whatever taste of sweetness you can give.

THE LAST TIME I SAW LOGAN

THE LIGHT TURNED GREEN, and I eased forward past the coffee shop where the skinny blond girl hanged herself. I turned left and then right in front of the pizza place near the bus stop where that older black man was shot in the head for no apparent reason. From there, I headed east up the first long block of small houses with their crumbling brick facades. My sponsor had lived in one of those: Danny Q., dead eight years from old age and a hard life he enjoyed leaving behind. Then came an even longer block, the one Danny warned me about, where a man might pull up to the curb, honk his horn twice, and have folks from at least three houses rush outside to fill his order for coke, pills, or whatever. That block claimed murders, too: shootings, stabbings, a bare-handed strangling, even a guy set on fire while he lay face down in the grass, hopped up out of his mind on smack. Of course, all of that happened a decade before the last time I saw Logan, back when I was in the program. The city and cops together had long since renovated these houses. *Renovated—*

that's how I thought about things like civil forfeiture, nighttime raids, and gray-skinned junkies dragged off in handcuffs that barely stayed on their bony wrists.

That neighborhood had changed. As I drove past, I knew the houses were owned by young lawyers and retired couples, as well as people like the events manager from the Civic Auditorium, and the Gerstler family that ran Gerstler Mortuary on the other side of town. Not even the Gerstlers, though, liked to talk about all the corpses that had come to rest, whether on purpose or by accident, in the area. That was the problem with reclaimed zones like this: folks could drive out the killers, paint over graffiti, and demolish rundown buildings, but they couldn't erase history or exorcise the ghosts.

I knew all about having a darker past. I overdosed to the point of a near-death experience three times. I committed petty crimes of the snatch-and-run variety. Twice the cops picked me up for DUI while I was stoned on Oxycontin, and I still felt thankful only the first charge stuck: a misdemeanor with its small fine and its year of unsupervised probation.

Shaking off the memories, I pulled up to the next STOP sign where I waited out a funeral procession moving perpendicular down Bradshaw Street. It wasn't the Gerstlers leading the way. I recognized the silver hearse from Pearl Funeral Home. The Pearls handled most of the poorer clients in this part of town, although I couldn't tell that from the line of fifty cars passing me with their hazard lights blinking and those little purple flags clicking against the air like baseball cards in the spokes of bicycle wheels. Most were high-dollar pickup trucks and sporty SUVs. There were a few rust buckets, but not many.

My Plymouth sputtered as I waited. It seemed nervous in the summer heat. I revved the gas to steady the engine, which brought me angry glances from mean-eyed men and women in the passing cars.

After the last vehicle eased by, I took my foot off the brake and drove the remaining four blocks toward the address I'd been given. Here were weathered rental houses in white wood or gray-green paneling. Many kept overgrown lawns in which I still imagined hidden bodies. About every third mailbox was torn down or leaning. Various folks stood in their thin driveways exchanging the clumsy handshake of a drug deal with strangers. The city's sanitizing hadn't made it this far yet.

Turning left onto War Street, I found a place to park along the curb. I was careful not to roll down my windows or honk my horn lest someone try to sell me dope.

After checking my surroundings, I stepped out of the car and headed for the dirty white box of a one-story house. Six-inch grass covered the small lawn, with a crabapple tree on the left side of the walkway. A mutt of some kind, brown spotted over white shag, was chained there, lying stretched on its forepaws and basking in what sunlight it could reach. It didn't bark or growl as I passed, but raised a wrinkled eyelid before relaxing again.

When I knew Logan Miller before, he referred to himself as *cat people*. He said he despised *dog people* because he thought they were brutal, ugly, and dumb like their beasts. I couldn't imagine Logan with a dog for a pet. It made me doubt I was in the right place, and also why I'd come at all.

At the door, I pressed the button but didn't hear a buzz or bell. So, I knocked. Twice. When I heard the locks clatter, I pulled the screen and waited as the main door opened in.

Logan stood on the other side, skinnier than I remembered and with his dark hair shaved down to a military fade. His mouth hung open, and I saw black spots where a few of his teeth should be. He wore a stained tee shirt and khaki cargo shorts that made him look like a safari guide on a bender.

When Logan raised his arm, he pointed a dark-metaled snub-nose .38 at my chest. It was an old-school cop gun, and Logan, with his record, could get five years' fed time just for holding it in his hand. "Fuck you, Lyle," he said, "you fucking prick!"

———— · ♦ · ————

I met Logan through a friend of a friend. That's the way it worked in dope circles. A girl I was seeing introduced me to a coworker who could get some pills. She, in turn, passed me off to a guy named Butch who knew people and earned his fix by making introductions. Butch hooked me up with Logan, and Logan had connections all over town: rednecks and hipsters, pseudo-businessmen in their cream shirts and silk ties, dirty cops, bikers, drag queens ... especially the queens. They had the best coke, and that was Logan's drug of choice before I came along.

The queens loved Logan. He sparkled under the flickering dancefloor lights as if his skin were made of glitter. He kept his hair dyed bright and styled in waves. He wasn't the tallest guy in the room, but he muscled up in the pecs and shoulders so he looked sort of tough, which kept most folks from messing with him. Not that it mattered. He'd scrap with anybody and hold his own. He had a temper, too. He caught his first felony for pistol-whipping a drunk football player who made the mistake of calling him *faggot* on the wrong night in an alley behind the Pyramid Club. I was there, and I saw him split the guy open, blood splashing up as if mud puddles stepped in by a heavy boot. Of course, I took off before the cops came. I wanted no part of that action. Logan didn't either. Malicious Wounding carried two to ten.

But that came later. In the beginning, I'd call him up once or twice a week, and we'd go on a scavenger hunt for pills: Oxycontin, Roxicet, Tylox, Percodan, or if those weren't available, Lortabs, Vicodin, maybe the occasional methadone wafer. If it was around, Logan could find it. I paid him a few bucks for the search or cut him a line from one of my pills after I crushed it. He'd snort it up, hand me the straw as if a pen he borrowed, and say, "Call me again *real* soon."

Back in those days, I was set. I had a hundred and thirty grand in the bank from an insurance settlement I earned by being in a crosswalk when a drunk in a beat-up Taurus decided to run a red light. That was a lot of money for a twenty-three-year-old fresh out of college with a useless degree in political science and a permanent limp where my hipbone and knee had been shattered, the knee almost turned to dust. That accident also paid me with my first taste of oxycodone. It wasn't long before I became a glutton.

It was the same with calling Logan. At first, I kept to my routine of calling once or twice a week. That soon became three or four times, and then every day. I'd buy enough pills to get me through a three-day weekend, and then end up doing them all before I went to bed on the first night. By the time I burned through the first half of my money, I was snorting at least four eighty-milligram tablets a day, and often a lot more than that.

It wasn't long before I didn't need to call Logan anymore, because he was always there. He hung out at my apartment downtown by the university, where we stayed fucked up until it was time to find more dope. Then, we headed out to every dive bar, coffee shop, hipster restaurant, and anywhere else he could think of, until we found what we needed. Nights, we usually ended up at the Pyramid Club. He strutted through the red double doors, dragging me with him past the bouncer without either of us paying the cover or collecting the glow-in-the-dark stamps on the backs of our hands. Then Logan went up to whichever drag queen came off stage—maybe the one made up to look like Cher in a fishnet body suit—and sneaked a quick kiss on the mouth. As he pulled away, he wiped off lipstick by using the back of his hand so he didn't look like the Joker from one of the Batman flicks. Then faux-Cher would say hello, calling Logan *Goosie*, which was his nickname for reasons he kept to himself. "Hey, slut," Logan would reply, tone always friendly and discreet. "You got any powder tonight? You got any pills?"

Those were long nights. They often ended with Logan crashing on my couch—or on my floor, if he couldn't make it any farther.

"**You evil fucker**," he said, waving his gun up and down like a conductor's baton.

I held my hands out in a pacifying gesture. "Calm down, man. You called me, remember?" It wasn't exactly true. He had looked me up on Facebook and sent a friend request, along with a message that read: *Lyle Brandt, as I live and breathe.* We traded a few messages after that, before he told me he was in trouble and asked if I'd come over to see him.

"Now I've got you right where I want you," he said.

"Hey, stay calm."

"Tell me I'm still beautiful," he said.

"What?"

"Tell me I'm still beautiful."

I didn't reply.

"Tell me, damn it."

I sighed. "I was in the program, you know. Those Narcotics Anonymous guys taught me that if you want to stay sober, you have to be brutally honest." My toes tensed, and I think I held my breath.

A grin crept over Logan's gap-toothed mouth, and he started to laugh.

"I mean," I continued, "you really let yourself go."

He lowered his arm and, with a sideways swing, tossed the .38 onto his battered blue love seat. Logan took three steps toward me and squeezed me in an embrace, pulling me into the house while my arms hung limp at my sides. Backing away, he shut the door and looked me over as if I were a model. "Well, you haven't changed at all, except for maybe that aw-shucks boy-scout look in your eyes. Not so hungry and desperate anymore."

He was right. I still wore the same dark tees under flannel shirts. I hadn't changed my hairstyle since I turned sixteen: center part, long bangs. I'd put on a few pounds, and I knew Logan could see that in my cheeks, but it wasn't that much of a difference. The main revision for me was that I'd been sober for almost a decade.

"I miss those days," he said.

"I don't."

"Sure you do. Brutal honesty, right?"

"Well, I miss my friends, and I miss the good times, but there were far more bad than good."

"Ain't it the truth?" he said. He ushered me over to the love seat and pushed me down next to his gun. "Can I get you something to drink? I've got Southern Comfort and orange juice. No, you were never much of a drinker."

"Thanks. I'm fine."

"Cool," he said. "Cool." He dropped down onto the floor at my feet and sat in the lotus position. It's then that I realized he didn't have any other furniture aside from a battered end table and a TV hanging from the wall. The carpet was beige and stained in waves so that it looked like the bottom of a shoe.

I felt uncomfortable with him sitting there, staring up at me, so I looked away. I glanced at the lone photo he kept in a frame on the end table. It was the two of us, glassy-eyed and wasted, surrounded by smiling queens in the alley outside the Pyramid Club. New Years' Eve, as I recall. Everyone was happy.

"You remember that?" he asked.

"Yeah. That is, I *don't* remember it, and that's what I remember about it."

———— • ♦ • ————

Logan tried to kiss me once. We were alone in my apartment, watching the Three Stooges on one of the rerun channels. We were high, of course. We were always high, or else in withdrawal. One or the other. A junkie's life.

The show went to a commercial break, and I said, "I can't believe that's still funny."

Logan didn't reply. Instead, I felt his eyes fixed on me with a lot of intensity, until he said, "You're all flushed." He placed a hand on my cheek. I let it rest there: a bandage, parts awkwardness and reassurance. Then he used that hand to pull my head around until his mouth was inches from mine.

I shook him off. "I'm not like that," I told him.

He backed away. "Sorry," he said, and we never spoke of it again.

———— • ♦ • ————

"**A**re you high right now?"

He rubbed his pale, bony knees where they jutted out from the hem of his shorts. "A little," he said. "Not much. One last fling before...."

"You're quitting?" I asked.

"I guess you could say that."

"Stop being so fucking cryptic. What's the deal? Why did you beg me to come over?"

"A little complicated," he said.

"Always is for people like us. But you know I'm clean now. Have been for a long time. So, you're making me nervous. Whatever's eating at you, spill it. If I can help you, I will. I'm not helping you get dope, though. I feel like I need to say that out loud."

"It's cool," he said. "You can't help me anyway. Not now."

"Shit, man. You sound like you're dying."

"Worse. I'm going back inside."

"Jail?"

"Prison."

I heard myself sigh. Inhaling again, I smelled a mix of perfume and onions. Looking around to avoid his gaze, I couldn't locate the source of the scent. Turning back, I said, "Okay, what did you do this time?"

"Snitch wore a wire. Caught me dealing out behind the club."

"The Pyramid?"

"No, the Circus. Pyramid's been gone for years. Anyway, it was just a gram of powder. My last bag. Lucky for me, too. When the cops patted me down, they didn't find anything else."

"But they got you on tape?"

"Yeah, audio."

I sighed again. "That's—what?—one to fifteen?"

"No, the audio was rough. My lawyer said the jury might not convict. She was able to get me a good deal. She set it up so I could plead to Conspiracy, and I wouldn't have to rat out or wear a wire on any of my friends. So, Conspiracy it is. Five flat."

"Another five years?"

"With good time, I'll kill it in two and a half—that is, as long as I don't take parole or get caught sucking dick on the rec yard." He tried to force a smile, but it came out crooked like the maw of a jack-o-lantern. "I'm on bond now. My sentencing's next week."

"Maybe the judge'll put you on probation."

He shook his head.

"No chance?"

"None. My lawyer made that clear."

"Which judge?"

"Hopkins."

"Oh, he's a shitheel."

"Exactly," he said. "That's exactly what I'm saying."

——— • ♦ • ———

When I was arrested for what should've been my second DUI, I had been off probation for about three weeks. The cop pulled me over for weaving in and out of my lane. He gave me a breathalyzer and determined I wasn't drunk, then took me in for a blood test, which I refused. That was like an admission of guilt, so I went straight to the Regional Jail. I spent four days there, waiting for my folks to cough up the five hundred bucks to a bondsman to bail me out. Almost but not quite long enough to detox from the Oxys. I spent nearly the whole time sitting on or kneeling over the steel toilet in my cell in the medical unit. I sweated through my tee shirt and orange jumpsuit, the sheets on my cot, even my socks. I felt grimy and smelled like deviled eggs.

When the guards finally let me out to take a shower, I ran into Logan just long enough to say hello. He was still waiting on his transfer to the penitentiary, and the nurses had him in medical with a suspected staph infection. He didn't have staph, he told me, but he was nice to the nurses, and they liked to give him a break from the general population every now and then because they could chat with him and not have to worry about him trying to get in their pants.

Overall, Logan looked clean and well-adjusted. I thought, *Damn, jail's done wonders for you.*

He couldn't say the same for me. "Get yourself together, Lyle," he told me. "You look like cat vomit on a shag rug." Those were the last words from him for almost a decade. They stuck with me even after my public defender somehow beat my charge.

I straightened up after that. Sure, there were a few slips along the way, but every time I fell off the wagon I heard his soft voice in my head: *You look like cat vomit on a shag rug.* That, along with the fact I'd spent all my settlement money and pawned everything of value I owned, was what I needed to keep me sober.

In a way, I owed Logan. His words were a kindness he didn't know he gave.

———— · ♦ · ————

"Had my teeth pulled," he told me. "They were bad anyway. I figured that if I'm going away for two and a half, I might as well make the state pay for some new ceramics."

"Makes sense. What about the hair?"

"Oh, they shave it for you anyway when you get to the pen. I forgot you never made it that far. They say it's to break you down, to show you you're nothing, but I think it's because they don't want you to look too pretty. For someone like me, it kind of helps. Being a queer on the inside's not the sausage party you'd think."

I shifted uncomfortably on the love seat. My leg had stiffened, and I knew it wouldn't be long before it began to ache. I felt tense as if I were the one on his way to the clink.

Logan didn't notice. He went on with his story, explaining how most of the cons didn't want to be around a gay man for fear they might be labeled as one. As for the rest, many just thought Logan was some kind of hooker—chatting him up, offering him goods from the prison commissary, then trying to sneak with him into the shower. Getting caught meant sixty days in the hole and up to two years' loss of good time. Even without getting caught, he said he was subject to be moved to another pod if a guard so much as imagined there might be something intimate going on. "The higher-ups are afraid I'll sue the prison and say I got raped," he said. "I could hang out with the other out-in-the-open queers, but you've never seen such a bunch of backstabbers. Competition, you know. Always causing so much drama."

"Pretty wild," I said, still shifting nervously.

This time Logan noticed. "You all right, man? Sure I can't get you a glass of water or whatever? I promise I won't offer you anything stronger."

"No. Thanks, but I got to go before too much longer. My old lady's waiting for me."

"Shit. I never thought to ask. You married?"

"Just seeing someone."

"How long?"

"A while."

"That's great, Lyle. That's great."

"So, listen. Why don't you tell me what you wanted? Why'd you beg me to come over? I asked once already, but you didn't answer."

"I wouldn't say *beg*," he said.

"Well, you said it on Facebook."

He shrugged. "I just ... don't have many friends anymore. We used to be friends. Are we still friends?"

I said, "Haven't seen you or heard from you in years, but yeah, yeah, we're friends. I mean, I'm not driving two hundred miles in a thunderstorm to get you dope ... to get *us* dope ... like in the old days. Still, you know what I'm saying."

"Would you write me letters?" he asked.

That threw me. "While you're locked up?" I said.

"It's lonely in there," he explained. "My mom and dad have never wanted anything to do with me and, like I said, I don't have many friends."

I thought about it and couldn't find a reason to tell him no.

"I understand if you don't want to, but..."

"It's cool," I said. "What address?"

"I'll be at the jail for a while. You'll have to look it up online." He hesitated, trying to read me. "Better yet, why don't you give me your address? Then I can write you first."

"Sure," I said.

We talked for half an hour after that, reminiscing about the good old days that weren't so good and the bad old days that were worse. We talked about his boyfriends and my girlfriends and our mutual friends or friends of friends from long ago. That was hard. It brought my head back to thoughts of death and ghosts.

Jerry, the icon of a bartender at the Pyramid Club: overdose.

Shauna, one of our dealers: overdose.

Elaine, who slept with me once and sold Logan coke: car wreck.

Kiwi, one of the queens—pretty and smooth even without makeup and while wearing street clothes: overdose. That one shocked me. Kiwi didn't do drugs back in our day. I guess it was the culture, though. Destiny. Logan said Kiwi's parents found the body slumped over on their porch swing, taken out by a cocktail of heroin and fentanyl. "Didn't have the looks anymore," Logan assured me. "Just another junkie on the nod."

After that, I didn't want to stay any longer. I made my excuses, and Logan nodded like a puppet with a weary hand inside. "That's fine," he said. "Really. I've got ... something to do, and I didn't want to do it with you here. Didn't want to test you anymore." Then he said goodbye. That was almost five years ago.

• ♦ •

He never wrote to me, and I never wrote him back. I doubt he even thought about it or remembered that I gave him my address. Likewise, his face rarely popped into my head.

I thought about him last night only because I heard his name spoken on the local news. It was said during video footage of a silver 1980s Pontiac Fiero so completely crushed that what remained of its fiberglass body resembled a ball of aluminum foil. There had been a chase over winding hillside roads before Logan missed a curve, bounced the Fiero off a concrete barrier, and rolled it half a dozen times, crumpling it against an oak.

The Trooper who'd been chasing Logan wiped away tears as he faced the camera. "I don't know why he ran," the cop said. "I just flashed him to tell him he had a broken taillight, and he took off. I'm speechless. I'm just..."

The video faded, replaced by a somber-eyed anchorman in a gray suit.

There was more about the incident in this morning's paper. The article mentioned Logan's past troubles with the law, but said he didn't have any outstanding warrants. No drugs were found in his car. The paper quoted his sister Martha who swore Logan was sober and had been for a few years now. Like the Trooper, she couldn't understand why he fled from a traffic stop.

It was all a mystery.

What threw me though, was that in almost two decades since Logan and I first met, he never mentioned that he had a sister. I wondered if she was kind to him, and if she wrote him letters while he was locked up. The newspaper couldn't tell me that, just like it couldn't explain to me why a man does the things he does, why he flips out or loses control, or why when people die the past looks brighter than it really is.

———— · ♦ · ————

THE POLICE ARTIST'S SKETCH

I.

LESTER RAISED THE KNIFE—A long pocket blade with a graphite handle molded to his palm as if a woman's breast. The edge eased through clumps of hair, back to front, not so much ripping as separating, the way careful hands might pull apart fine linens fresh from the dryer. Brown tumbleweeds rolled down his cheeks, bounced from his shoulders and fell to the bathroom floor or landed in the faux-marble sink. He watched himself in the mirror as he cut. At first, he resembled a pretty-boy rock'n'roller in some second-rate bar band. Now he just looked deranged, maybe a little diseased, the remnants of his flowing curls now a burned forest with smoldering ghosts of trees left barely standing. Later, he'd bulldoze the remains with a razor, maybe take off his perfectly shaped eyebrows, too. He needed this negative metamorphosis, the butterfly becoming a caterpillar.

"Damn it," he grunted as the honed steel nicked his scalp. This blade was one inch longer than its brother that he'd thrown away, and the added length was enough to catch skin. A quick trickle of blood descended. He reached for toilet tissue, balled it up and pressed it to the wound, holding it there, squeezing, waiting, looking all the more ridiculous. *I'm going to be ugly*, he thought, although ugly was exactly what he wanted.

As if to remind himself why, he glanced down at the folded newspaper on the toilet seat. There, in neat charcoal turned to printer's ink, was his likeness. A striking sketch, it caught his angelic good looks, his small, tight face, his princely chin, his somber eyes that, even in the picture, seemed to hint at blue. It captured him so much better than yesterday's photo from the surveillance camera that came out grainy and blurred and made him resemble Jesus in a gray windbreaker, but also could've been a picture of a scarecrow or a cardboard cutout of a two-toed sloth. The sketch was devastating in its accuracy. That sketch could put him in chains.

II.

He still bore the scar on his thumb where he cut himself wielding the other knife. He was the only one he injured, though not the only one he frightened with his actions. He hadn't planned anything—pulling the weapon, waving it about, robbing the register. It surprised him as much as the old salesman he threatened.

Lester got out of the taxi and handed the driver five dollars. Scanning the contents of his wallet, he saw twenty-three left—two tens and three ones. He couldn't do much with that. He had two *Visa* cards that were still active, but he didn't know how close they were to being maxed. Would he have enough? He doubted it. He was too broke to spend a few days at the beach. He couldn't afford to be stranded here. He was just passing through on his way to a better place, a better life, and now this.... His beat-up baby blue *Ford* crapped out around 3rd Street and Empire Avenue. It was the alternator, he figured, though maybe the battery died with it in the collateral damage.

Now, he stood in front of the auto parts store with little hope and less money. But he had to go in. He had to see....

Light poured through the chain store's wide glass windows and doors, a blazing chandelier in the twilight. The shop would close soon, he knew, so he needed to hurry. Lester could tell from the empty parking lot and the view through those windows that no customers remained inside. He stumbled up the walk like a mosquito drawn by the neon column of a zapper. He couldn't escape his need or his fate.

The doors didn't open automatically. They were heavy security doors, steel framed, with wide, flat handles. Those doors opened out, reminding Lester of the entrance to a castle's great hall in one of those *Lord of the Rings* movies. He tugged, getting the weight of them, then stretched them open and stepped through into the light.

The first things he noticed were rows upon rows of steel shelves stacked with batteries, water pumps, sparkplugs, windshield wipers and the like. Some items sat out in the open. Others were buried in boxes with line-art drawings on the front.

Lester inhaled, expecting the grease smells of a garage, but the only odors were bleach and faint traces of cigarette smoke where some rebellious employee stole a puff in a darkened back room.

He took a few steps farther in, allowing the doors to fall shut behind him.

"Hey there, sugar," said a soft but bright female voice, startling him from his reverie.

Lester turned to his right to see who spoke.

III.

He held up the folded newspaper, staring at his uncanny likeness. *It had to be her*, he thought. *She's the one that saw me clearly.* Lester hadn't yet made the critical decision when he walked into the store. He had made eye contact. He thought he'd even smiled. She saw him in all his angelic glory—the way so many women saw him, attracted to him, memorizing him by pieces like names of generals for a history exam. For years he had turned them all away, not expecting the miserable hour to come when he would find himself alone. So, he could forgive himself now for a flirtatious grin or a pair of wandering eyes. It's what came later that made this single moment seem somehow inappropriate. *Yes, it was definitely her.*

Lester slung the newspaper across the room. It struck a fat white lamp that wobbled once and righted itself, though its shade developed a penitent nod.

He remembered her: hair the tint of snowdrifts under an arc lamp at night, green eyes piercing and revealing like blips on a radar screen, tiny shoulders covered with a plain white blouse—

they peeked out from beneath her uniform's red vest. She wore black stretch pants and black sneakers, too. She was five and a half feet at most, and small-framed except for a little heaviness in her thighs, which Lester also wasted too much time noticing. *She saw me*, he thought. *She can't forget me.* Now, after all this, he couldn't forget her either. They were bound—a pharaoh and his concubine sent together into the afterlife.

IV.

"Hey there, sugar," she said.

Lester turned to see.

"What you need tonight, honey? Something small, I hope. We're about ready to lock up for the night." Just then, he noticed the mop in her hand, its handle red as her vest. "Better tell me what we can help you with. Best not waste any time."

Lester glanced at her nametag riding the small hump of her left breast. *Anna*, it read. "Well, Anna," he told her, "I need an alternator for a 1984 *Ford*..."

"Ooh," she interrupted, pouting with her thin, pink lips. "That's a big buy. Too big for me. You'll have to talk to Jasper."

"Where's he?"

"All the way in the back by the other register."

Lester scanned the aisles. They looked like rows of tunnels that ran for miles, or vast steel catacombs of robot crypts.

"Head on back. You can't miss him. He's the only other person in the store."

"Thanks, Anna," Lester said, then turned to go.

"Sure thing, honey," she said. Every word she spoke sounded like an invitation.

V.

Lester pulled off his tee shirt and tossed it over the back of a yellow-and-white deck chair. He stripped to his black boxers that he hoped were long enough and dark enough to pass for swim trunks. Then he eased into the icy water, down the plaster steps at the shallow end. Lester wasn't used to staying in the kind of motel that would have a pool. Though the water was dirty and coated with the corpses of spiders and insects, he still looked forward to the soothing motions of the water as he swam or floated, as he tried to forget.

He made it in up to his waist and paused to build up his resolve, soon flattening out and diving under the surface. When he reemerged, a boy was staring at him from the ledge of the deep end where the diving board should have been. He looked to be about ten or eleven, wearing new dark blue jeans and a white tee with *WWJD?* emblazoned on the front. He had a fat face beneath an upturned bowl of greasy brown hair. For some reason, Lester thought of the kid from *The Omen*, although that notion quickly passed. "You look like Uncle Fester," the boy said, his voice squeaky and sharp, but friendly.

"Uncle who?"

"Uncle Fester. You know, from *The Addams Family?*"

"Oh, right. Does that make you Pugsley?"

The kid laughed and shook his head. "No, I'm smarter than that."

"But as mischievous, I bet." Lester dove back down and swam below the surface all the way to the deep end. When he came back up, he saw the kid still there on the ledge, having sat there with his legs crossed. "So, who are *you*?" he asked.

"I'm Just..."

"Just what?"

"No, Just. Short for Justin. That's my name."

VI.

The guy in back wore the same red vest over a white dress shirt. He was older, his thin, square head covered with a choppy carpet of gray hair. He smiled, showing off his massive overbite and a missing incisor on the left side. "That's a fine model, but a pretty old mistress," he said. "You'd be better off trading her in for a younger gal." When Lester squinted but didn't reply, the old fellow—his nametag read *Jasper*—chuckled. "Well, you want a little of that plastic surgery to get her hot and running for a lick, well, I guess I can fix you right up when it comes down to it. An alternator, you say?"

"That's right."

"We probably got one. Best expect to clean a mighty layer of dust off it."

"If you got it at all, I'll be happy."

"Sure, sure. Let's check the inventory." Jasper went to the computer and started tapping the screen. Every touch brought a soft beep. Jasper's head moved up and down, scanning the monitor, reading every line of text and examining each picture, all the while his fingers tapping, tapping, tapping. "Well, what do you know? Says here we got a pair. That's a surplus, far as I'm concerned, but mister, you're in luck."

"Fantastic," said Lester. "How much?"

Jasper looked at the screen, looked at Lester, then looked at the screen again. He shook his head. "Says here it's one-seventy-nine ninety-nine."

"Ouch," Lester grunted, squinted. "A hundred and eighty bucks. That's a mint."

"Yes, indeed. Can't be helped. The price is the price."

"Right."

"So, you want it? It's in inventory. Have to go in the back and dig it out. Say the word."

Lester thought about it. Would he have enough on the credit card? Would he have enough on both cards put together? If he bought it, did he have enough tools in the truck to do the work himself? He couldn't be sure. What a bind he was in. It was as if someone tied him to a tree in the middle of a lonely wood and left him there to starve or be eaten by wolves. "Don't guess I have any choice," he said.

The older man nodded, then touched the screen of his monitor to clear it. There was a loud click from underneath. "Oops," he said. The cash drawer slid open. It was filled with trays fat from twenties, tens, fives and whatever lay below. "Darnedest thing. Hate it when that happens."

Lester pretended not to notice. But he did. He noticed. He couldn't help it. He thought, *Haven't these people ever heard of a safe?*

VII.

"You forgot something." The boy sat cross-legged on the ledge. His dirty bangs clung like ivy to his forehead. When Lester glanced up at him from the pool, the kid looked like a baby Buddha haloed by cyan from the clear sky.

"What did you say?" Lester asked, treading water to keep his mouth from going under.

"You forgot something."

"I did?"

"Something important."

Lester's mind raced. *Does this kid know something?* he wondered. How did he figure it out? Who was he? What was he trying to do? Maybe the boy really wanted to help. Lester stopped kicking for a moment, and his whole head dipped under the water. Breaking the surface again, he shook left and right like a mutt to clear beads of water and the chaos of his thoughts. He regained his composure and his balance and said, "Okay, Just, what did I forget?"

The boy smiled. "You forgot to ask me what my shirt means."

Lester laughed, relieved, until he choked on a mouthful of water. Then he said, "I know what it means. I've seen the letters before."

"Not these letters," the boy said.

"What do you mean?"

"They're special letters. My mom said so."

"Oh yeah?"

"Yeah."

"What does *she* say they mean?"

"What would *Just* do?" he said.

Again, laughter. "I think I like your Mom. And what, pray tell, *would* Just do?"

The kid smiled back. "Anything I want."

VIII.

There was a moment—just a blink—while he was still innocent. He chewed on his lip and felt himself sweat under his arms. He could smell himself, soured with anxiety. He heard his inner voice pleading, urging, browbeating him, demanding he shout, "Danger! Run away! There's a bad man in your store!" He couldn't spit those words out, although he begged himself in a quieter voice to walk casually toward the exit, leave the auto parts store and never look back. He didn't even need to tell old Jasper to forget the alternator. All he had to do was turn and go. Just vamoose, vanish, fly off into the night, a mosquito unable to get himself drunk on blood.

"Wait here," said Jasper. "I'll get that for you and be right out."

Lester watched him go. As soon as the old clerk disappeared through the doorway, Lester drew his hand back, reaching into a pocket for his knife.

IX.

Lester swam a couple dozen laps beneath the surface, knifing through the dirty blue with graceful, wide-armed strokes. Submerged, breath held, eyes closed, he knew peace. He was free of his thoughts and free of his crimes. He could've been back in the womb, swimming for life, racing toward the world that would corrupt him.

Later. Another day. For now ... serenity.

When he came up at last, the boy was there again. Something the color of hotdog chili stained his shirt. He held a red *Big Gulp* cup with both hands and steadily sucked on the straw.

"You're back," said Lester.

The kid shrugged and slurped his soda.

"Where'd you run off to?"

"*Seven-Eleven* down the street," Just told him, adding after a pause, "I stole ten dollars out of your pants. I didn't think you'd mind." He pointed to the wad of clothes heaped up on a deck chair.

Lester's initial dumbfounded expression turned into a smirk. He really couldn't be mad at the boy. Besides, it was already stolen money. He had picked up a couple grand in the robbery. He could afford to share a little bit. "Only ten, right?"

"You shouldn't leave it lying around like that. The next fellow might not be so nice."

"I'll keep that in mind. Did you bring the change back at least?"

"Do you think I'd tell you if I did?"

"I guess not. But what if I told your mom?"

"Told me *what*?"

Lester spun around to see her coming through the gate, her flowing ginger hair blurring into the umber wood behind the wire-mesh fence. She looked thirty, maybe a little older. Her face was taut from a hard life or too much worry. Still, it was lovely. It had this plainness to it. He knew right off that she had never been a cheerleader, but neither had she lacked for admirers. She wore a purple top that rose off the midriff—a younger woman's shirt. Her belly was brown and smooth, an amethyst peeking out from her navel. Her shorts were white, glowing like moonlight through mist against her thin, tanned legs. Lester saw a lonely strand of violet rising above the waistband on her right side.

"Well?" she said. "Somebody want to fill me in?"

X.

He withdrew the knife with his left hand. His fingers twitched too much. He couldn't unfold the blade one-handed so, bringing his right arm around, he pulled the steel spike free. It was fine and hard and felt as big as a scimitar in his grip, though it was the smallest blade he owned. He shifted the handle to his right hand and carried it behind his back—waiting, waiting, waiting. He already knew he'd go through with it. The devil is the god of accidents, he knew, and the spirit from some black hell had opened that register to show him his way out.

XI.

It didn't pay to be so observant all the time. He often fixed on some detail most folks overlooked—some feature small as hints of lipstick pink from rose petals scattered across the lawn in the gray after a storm, or large as the expression on a woman's face when she knows he knows what she did and knows he's leaving. He focused on that tiny indigo hyphen drawn aslant across her hip. It inspired him to imagine the shape of her in nothing but those purple panties. What were they beneath the strap? Satin? Lace? If he slid his hand down the front of her shorts, would he feel some silky patch already warm? He pictured it, painted it, sketched it in all its animal glory.

Lester kicked his legs faster to cover up the flutter in his groin. "So, you're Just's mother?" he said, to say *something*.

"Kelly," she replied, holding out a hand as if he could shake it from the middle of the pool. She moved that hand toward Just and waved him toward the gate. "Just, honey, go on back to the room now. Let me have a chat with your new friend."

"Sure, Mom. Go easy on him. He's not a bad guy. Not too careful with money, and that bald head looks dumb, but he's not a meanie. I can tell."

"Thanks, I guess," said Lester.

"Thank you, Mister, for the lunch."

"You bought him lunch?" said Kelly.

"Sort of," said Lester.

Kelly watched the boy leave through the gate, then turned back to the man in the pool. "I told you my name. You plan on telling me yours?"

"Shit," said Lester. "Sorry."

"Uh huh."

"I'm Lester. Lester Corey."

"Well, Lester Corey, my son said you're not a meanie, and that carries a lot of weight. It's certainly good enough for me. I know we just met and all, but I can see you want to ask me out. Let's say seven o'clock. That work for you?"

Lester shook his head to flick away a few droplets of water. "Sounds wonderful," he said, "I think." It took him a minute for what she had suggested to sink in. "What did you mean you can see?"

She pointed into the pool.

He followed the aim of her finger and looked down. His prick, half erect and still rising, danced free from the loose flap of his boxers. It floated there like a submarine aimed for its ascent to the surface. "Oh, Jesus," he said. He reached down to cover himself and adjust his drawers. His head sank beneath the waterline. When he came back up, Kelly was walking away—laughing and shaking her head. "Wait," he said, gurgling a little on dirty pool water. "If you're serious, where do I find you?"

She turned, smiled, laughed a little more. "Thirty-three," she said. "Third floor by the ice machine."

"What about your boy?"

"Don't worry about Just. He's young, but he knows how to take care of himself."

XII.

Lester hid by the entrance to the stock room. His hand trembled holding the knife behind his back, nearly letting it drop. He squeezed the graphite handle. It felt to him like nothing was there, so he clenched it again and again.

Old Jasper came out carrying a box with the alternator inside. He held it out tenderly as if it were a birthday cake.

Lester lunged at him from behind. He lifted the knife and touched steel to the man's throat. "I'm sorry about this, mister, but I need that money."

Jasper dropped the box and let out a gasp that wasn't quite a scream so much as a cross between a whimper and a prayer.

"I'm sorry," Lester said again. He was so nervous he held the knife backward. The flat of it braced against the flesh of Jasper's throat. Lester was shaking too much. To steady the blade, he pressed with his thumb and sliced it open on the honed edge. He nearly cried out himself, but he managed to hold that in as blood spilled around the metal.

Old Jasper didn't notice that the knife was backward. The sudden warmth and wetness of blood on his neck frightened him all the more. He tensed and stood still until Lester eased forward, then moved with him one slow step at a time.

"I hate doing this to you. If only I didn't need it so much..."

The clerk reached out a thin, gray finger toward the touch screen. An instant later, the drawer shot open with a click that sounded loud as a trumpet in Lester's ears but was really rather quiet and muffled by the hum of the air conditioner and exhaust fans overhead.

"Grab a bag," said Lester. He stared at the stacks of money. There was probably more in that drawer than he'd have gotten away with if he'd robbed a bank. "Put it in there," he said. "Put it all in there."

XIII.

He eased her through the doorway of his motel room. She wore a flowered summer dress that rose above her knees, with no stockings underneath and no socks but only a pair of cheap white canvas sneakers on her feet. She purred as he slid his hands up her tight thighs, while she reached up behind her to stroke the stubble atop his head. He kissed her neck, and she sighed. He breathed on her earlobe, and she moaned, pulling his head to her. His hands skipped over the straps of her panties to find a grip on her sides. She eased a foot between his legs, using it to close the door.

They had spent a pleasant evening together. He bought her a steak dinner using blood-stained bills. He took her to a movie—something about a young pregnant woman falling in love with a gay man. They talked a great deal about her husband who left her and his wife who made *him* leave *her*. They joked about how maybe the two were off together somewhere, perhaps chained and being thrown by natives into a raging volcano. He made her smile often with his sarcasm, and she stole all his guilt away, if only for a little while.

Later, they walked along the beach, already kissing, holding, playfully groping, as if their whole relationship existed only in this moment, this infatuated pause from reality. Lester knew there was no black and white for him. A man can be good and bad at the same time. For now, he was so good, as good as he could be in her embrace.

His hands moved to her middle, thumbs rubbing delicate circles. She arched slightly as if he had found the true center of her. He arched with her, taut jeans riding the valley her buttocks framed. His fingers reached the ring in her navel at the same time—amethyst, he remembered. Then, recalling more, he ran his hands down her front, seeking the purple he had imagined on her. The panties were lace, he felt now, coarse and latticed. He pressed deep, rubbing as if to warm his hands under a faucet. Kelly mewed and gasped. He kissed her neck again and again until she turned her lips to him. Then he devoured them. They tasted like grapes and tobacco. He smelled those flavors too, pictured her beside him, the two of them smoking cigarettes in a vineyard by moonlight. How innocent he felt, and how forgiven. This was no robbery; it was a gift.

Finally, she spun to meet him just before their bodies found the bed with its thin off-white cover. Kelly started to kiss him but pulled back. He expected her to say something like "I don't usually do this," or maybe, "We're moving too fast." What she actually said was, "It's a shame there's no room service. I like my coffee black and my eggs over-easy." Then she kissed him, as her fingers probed the waistband of his jeans.

XIV.

He froze, trying to decide about the alternator. Should he take it? Leave it where it lay? He had revealed too much: the make and model of the truck, that it was broken and how. The cops would find it soon enough. Then what? It wasn't registered to him, but the license could be traced back to Tennessee and the crusty old badger who sold it for five hundred bucks, cash on wood. Had Lester told the man his name? He didn't remember. *Hell*, he thought, *that truck's cursed, and that guy deserves the hassle coming his way.* "Leave it," he muttered.

Old Jasper flinched. His eyes swore he didn't know what was expected of him.

Lester grabbed the bag full of money out of Jasper's hand. Then he ran. He ran and ran and ran…

XV.

As Lester crept through the doorway, he tried not to disturb her, but a brilliant, reddish-pink, stained-glass mural of sun and sky bulldozed past him, setting her alight. "Mmmm," she moaned. She rested on her belly, a lone sheet covering one side of her. Leg, buttock, shoulder blade and arm lay exposed as the bright hues ignited all around her. She groaned again softly and covered her eyes with her forearm and crashing waves of her hair. "What time is it?"

"Early."

"Rrrr."

He sat beside her on the bed. His left hand carried a cardboard tray with three Styrofoam cups, his right a large, brown paper bag with a logo on the front. A folded newspaper snuggled under his arm. "I borrowed your car," he said.

That roused her. "You what?"

He rattled the bag, careful not to spill the drinks in his other hand. "Over-easy," he said. "Coffee, black." He paused for a breath before adding, "The keys were in your purse."

Kelly squinted, almost scowling. "You're as bad as Just. Take whatever you want whenever you want it."

He leaned down and kissed her, pulled back and placed the tray of drinks on a nightstand. The bag went beside it, followed by the paper. "Yes, I guess I do. I'm a man full of want and need and hunger, maybe a little darkness sometimes. Do you hate me for it?"

She moved crabwise into a sitting position, the sheet falling away. Her breasts were small and loose, pale and beckoning. She didn't answer at first.

"How can you hate me? I brought you eggs and coffee. I brought you breakfast in bed."

Another moment. Finally, a hint of a grin.

"Something for your boy, too. I hope he likes pancakes."

"He loves pancakes. But that better not be orange juice. He drinks his coffee black, the same as me."

Lester feathered a hand from her hip all the way up to the unnamed indentation where breast became her underarm. His blood warmed and skin cooled. His heartbeat sped and slowed, raced and whispered. He loved how easily she forgave him.

XVI.

He ran down the center aisle, clutching the bag in front of him, knife behind his back, blood dripping every few steps to spatter the white tiles. It took seconds but felt like days. Lester thought he'd never reach the door. And then he did. And....

The door was open. There stood Anna, mop in one hand, the door held with the other. She beamed at him with wide lips and perfect teeth. Her smile didn't seem the least bit artificial. "Come back and see us soon," she said.

Lester didn't slow, though in his mind he paused, hammered by her words. More seconds passed, an hour, a day, a year. Then he was by her, out in the night, picking up speed, and running ... anywhere, everywhere, nowhere—the direction didn't matter.

He was already lost.

XVII.

"This looks just like you."

His heart skipped. He coughed out a cloud he had inhaled from Kelly's menthol cigarette. He sat fully clothed in bed, one arm draped around her bare shoulders. "What did you say?"

"There's a picture in here. It looks like you."

Lester didn't want to see it, but he couldn't keep from glancing down when Kelly waved the newspaper in front of him. There was a sketch, an artist's rendering. It really did resemble him, bald head and all.

"It even has a little mark like that nick on your noggin. I think it's meant to be a tattoo."

The headline read, *"Police Release Artist's Sketch of Deer Beach Rapist."*

It wasn't him. *My God*, he thought. It really wasn't! Suddenly he began to laugh, startling Kelly, who glared at him with eyes screwed up and awkward. He handed her the cigarette and freed his other arm, using both thumbs to wipe his eyes. What he had thought was him wasn't him, and what he had thought was laughter wasn't laughter at all.

XVIII.

He ran on through the night, down strange and dirty avenues, around curves, and onto side streets even the city's dwellers probably didn't know existed. He crossed backyards, stumbled through gardens. He negotiated black patches of woods that would've seemed so out of place if he stopped to think about it. He didn't. His mind was elsewhere.

Over and over, he saw the girl, Anna. Her pretty eyes, her hair, her smile so like a prayer for the long-since damned. "Come back and see us soon," she had said. She didn't *know*. The distance between the front register and the back kept her ignorant of all the crimes in his heart. He wondered what she'd think when she found out. He imagined how terrified she'd be, and how grim that beautiful smile would turn. Lester shivered. So easily a man can break a woman, he thought, and so quickly he regrets.

How long had he been moving? He found the beach and slowed to a stagger. He went on, stumbling every few steps, all the while imagining and hurting, remembering and regretting. The money was one thing, but Anna was something else. He hadn't hurt a woman before, other than by bouts of aloofness and sarcasm. Never like this. This was the Fall of Man. It was the teeth of the shark as they tear at a swimmer's leg. He had poisoned her with bad deeds. Now he hated himself for his brutality.

"Forgive me," he whispered, stopping to stare at the moon above that ominous black ocean. "Damn me!" he shouted, tossing his knife as far out into the water as he could. He wished his arm were stronger, wished the knife would carry farther and farther, up and up, to strike that jaundiced, evil face in the sky.

XIX.

He told her everything, crying and repenting, shaking and wishing all manner of torment on himself. She cried, too, her tears like a hundred coins thrown into a well by travelers praying for things unlikely to come true. She held him close, burying his face in her neck or the groove between her breasts. She tried not to show how shocked she was, or how she suddenly loved him like a husband she already knew she had to lose. "There there," she told him, repeating the words as if they meant something.

"I don't know what to do," he said, in a tone that also implied, "I don't know what I've done." Then he added, "I don't have any right to ask this question."

She stroked his stubbly scalp.

"If I were in prison, would you come visit me?"

She wiped away a tear with the knuckle of her thumb. Was it his or hers? She wasn't certain.

"I'm sorry," he told her. "No right. I have no right."

"It's okay," she said.

"We had such a wonderful evening, didn't we?"

"It was special."

"I didn't mean to drag you into this."

"There there."

"It was the sketch. It was too much."

"There there."

"I couldn't handle it."

"There there. There there. There there."

He raised his head and started to say more, but she stopped him with a finger to his lips. Then, she leaned in and kissed the backs of his eyelids as if he were a child, as if he were Just after suffering from nightmares. Silence carried moments into minutes. The crying stopped, though the holding lingered. At last, he told her, "There's something else. The restaurant ... where I went to get your eggs...."

"Yes?"

"It's there ... right before the auto parts place."

Kelly sighed, nodded, petted his ear and the back of his neck.

"I drove right past it. Did you know there's a Sheriff's detachment not half a mile down the road? And, after that, another half mile takes you to the Interstate. Did you know that? From there, a man could go anywhere—another city, another state, another life."

This confused her. What did he mean? Was he asking for advice? For permission? She wasn't sure what to tell him. "There

there," she said. "There there." Her hand fell from his neck. She didn't know what she was doing until her fingers found his groin.

XX.

Sunlight tightened the skin of his face, and his eyes blurred, staring across the sand. He wanted a last look and a last chance to inhale that salty but sour beach smell that meant freedom. Whatever happened now, he was a captive to his fate. Bonds of steel or flesh or love or trust or the whims of some angry god—he was a prisoner to *something*.

Behind him, Kelly leaned into the backseat of her silver *Taurus*, checking Just's seatbelt as he squirmed a little, alternately smirking and staring down at the football game on his handheld *Nintendo*. "Okay, baby, we'll be off in a minute." She ruffled his hair, then backed out of the car, closing the door behind her. For the first time since Lester saw her, she looked like a wife and mother, wearing a white beach shirt and baggy white pants. Her hair was pulled back into a ponytail that protruded from a plain, white hat. She wore no make-up, and she looked somehow older than she had before. To Lester, that look was comforting.

Kelly went to him and kissed him. The bill of her hat tapped him on the forehead. "Are you ready?" she said.

"No," he told her.

She nodded. She understood.

"Have you decided?" he asked her.

"Where I'm taking you?"

"Yes. What's it to be?"

She turned from him, looking out across the sand and, farther still, across the water. The seeming forever of it calmed her, allowed her to put off the hard choice he had left to her. "Let's just drive," she told him. "We'll decide when we have to. The station or the Interstate? Let's not jinx ourselves by answering too soon."

BUSTED STRAIGHT

"**B**ULL DUG UNDER THE fence again." Pop pointed to a hole in churned earth beneath the wire mesh. It looked about a foot and a half wide and six inches deep—gaping enough for anything to crawl through. "We'll have to fix that."

"Sure, Pop," I said, knowing he wouldn't remember it. His mind worked like a camera's lens, only catching whatever happened to be in frame. "Get right on it."

"Good ole Bull never could stay put."

"Not a chance," I agreed. "Too much fox in his blood." I remembered the phrase as something Pop used to say before Bull died almost twenty years ago. Bull wasn't part fox. His name stood for bulldog, which he also wasn't. I pictured a mutt that could've been spaniel, hound, or an oversized, floppy-eared rat Pop mistook and adopted.

I moved Pop along the fence line, the graves of his eyes taking in everything, his thin, skeletal face pale and bluish in the morning light. I didn't correct him about Bull or the hole which had been put there months ago by a raccoon or opossum. Pop didn't recall much these days—not my kids Jan and Luanne who were off at college, not my ex-wife Sheila who was off in the head. He knew he used to drive a truck for the coal companies and that he bussed tables once as a teenager. Dementia took almost everything else, filling in gaps with black-suited demons and other colorful characters Pop saw dancing on the lawn.

Sometimes, on a peaceful day like this, he remembered Mom. "Zack," he said, "where's Caroline's apple tree?" He pointed to a circle of dirt where a young tree used to sprout tiny fruit that none of us ever ate. Pop uprooted the thing after Mom died. He burned it branch by branch and log by log in the fireplace, despite it being the middle of August and the air conditioner roaring to keep pace. "I think the tornadoes came and sucked it right up."

"Could be, Pop."

"Caroline's gonna be pissed. She'll raise holy hell about it."

"Uh huh. You know Mom."

"Lucky them funnels missed the house," he said. "You'd be sending me messages through the Devil's Express."

My brother Ted would've laughed to hear him say that, but I hated the phrase. I'd heard it enough since Pop's dementia kicked in. It brought up the one thing he never forgot: the time he gutted a man in Charleston. He got in a fight over a woman. Not Mom. The one before her. Even with Alzheimer's eating away at his brain, Pop still obsessed about the killing. He could recite every line of dialogue he and Jimbo Duggan spoke, and he *did* ... far too often for my taste.

"Now, Conway," Jimbo said, "I didn't know you was still seeing her. Angie told me you two broke up." Jimbo was naked and covered neck to ankle in blue jailhouse tattoos. Pop could describe all of them, especially the five-card hand of poker over Jimbo's heart—not the usual four aces and a king, but a busted straight: two, three, four, six, queen. Duggan, older than Pop, had been in the pokey much of his life, but he'd been out for a while, and now his prison muscles had gone soft.

"I already sent Angie out the door," Pop told him, "bare-assed, just like you."

"Ain't right, Conway."

"You wanted me to throw rose petals and escort you all down the aisle?"

"No, I wanted you to go fuck a pig!"

When telling the story, Pop usually added as an aside: *Can you believe that, Son? He was making me a pig fucker!*

When Jimbo lunged, Pop's hunting knife came so fast neither man saw a glint of steel.

I told the cops he said he'd kill me, Pop sometimes added. *Only thing that kept the murder charge off me.*

He spent eight years in Moundsville on voluntary manslaughter. How Pop came out a better man, I never understood. I'd read some horrible stories about what happened at that place before the state shut it down. I couldn't imagine Pop experiencing anything but brutality. Luckily, he didn't remember any of *that*.

Ted and I didn't learn about Pop's history until we were in high school. We knew he was twenty years older than Mom, and we'd seen his blue tattoos: a cobra on his wrist, a dagger on his shoulder blade. To us, he was just our father. He kept us clothed and fed, bought us presents every Christmas, took us to football practice. Later, he co-signed our student loans to get me to college and Ted all the way through law school, putting up his house as collateral. He was good to us, even after Mom passed.

I was seventeen—two years older than Ted—when she lost control of her car and rolled it down an embankment. The crash mangled her body, severing one arm and crushing her skull.

We hadn't seen Pop cry before. Nor had we heard him cuss. Now both flowed out of him as if he couldn't make up his mind between sorrow and rage. That night, burdened, Pop told us about his past. "Caroline kept me in line," he said. "She met a bad man at a bad time in his life, and she mopped it all away like dirt on the linoleum."

Neither of us knew what to say. It hurt to have lost her, but now we understood that she'd been the heroine of our father's story, too. And to watch Pop sob and swear and, that night, drink brown liquor for the first time since I'd been born—we broke down and gulped that bourbon with him until Ted went puking in the toilet and Pop started giving me life advice.

"Two things," my father told me. "First, women are like a hand of poker. Sometimes a weak ace turns out to be good enough, but it's always the ones you think strongest that rob you of everything you've got."

"Sure, Pop," I said.

"Second thing..." He paused, eyes glazed over, and lost his thoughts.

"What's the second thing, Pop?"

"If you ever kill a man, right or wrong, don't get caught."

• ♦ •

We walked around to the back of the house. Pop didn't have a backyard, just a rocky hillside sloping up into dark woods of pine and oak. The path between hill and house was muddy, with even the walkway stones covered. Everything smelled oily and fishlike.

"Where we going, Son?" he asked.

"Just taking a walk, Pop. Doc said you need fresh air once in a while..."

"He did not!" The sudden anger startled but didn't shock me. He often reacted that way to things folks talked about that he couldn't remember.

"...and exercise."

"Well, nobody told *me*!"

"Doc was out here just yesterday, Pop." I'm not sure why I argued. It'd be easier if I agreed with whatever he said and just pretended. I couldn't do it. Maybe some part of me still believed it might reach some part of him.

"Nobody told *me*," he repeated, sounding less angry and a little bit afraid.

I put a hand on his shoulder, and he flinched. I wasn't sure if he was reliving past trauma or just startled in that moment by the unexpected contact. It could be hard to tell the difference. "You okay, Pop?"

He stopped and looked at me as if I were a stranger.

"What's the matter?"

"I don't know," he said. "Something."

I hated these times most. If he lost himself in his memories, at least that made sense. I understood it. These in-between pauses were like sensing ghosts in another room—more doubt and discomfort, less terror, although that too seemed imminent. I wanted to turn on the lights and make our hearts feel safe and calm again.

I wondered if Ted felt that way. He could laugh about Pop's condition. He called it "Time Machine Syndrome," or said "If he's gotta get stuck in another part of his life, I'm glad it's a happy one most of the time."

Not sure what else to do, I nudged Pop onward.

"Old Bull," he said, as if reliving something specific. He didn't elaborate, though, and we kept moving.

Looking over my shoulder, I saw Joe the day nurse watching us through the rear window. Young, stocky, and dressed in maroon hospital scrubs, Joe wore his hair buzzed and looked more like a soldier for some foreign nation than a nurse. His cheeks were gaunt, but his arms muscular as if both designed for the jobs he had to do. He treated Pop with kindness and kept him from accidentally burning down the house or sleeping too long in his own excrement. Even so, Joe still drove a Mustang as if he were once the cool kid in school and never wanted to forget that feeling.

He waved to us through the window.

I waved back.

Pop looked at me funny and said, "What's wrong with your arm?"

Ted and I split the cost of Pop's twenty-four-hour care. It was the least we could do. Killer or not, Pop had been a perfect father to us. We wanted to let him live out his days in his own house. We didn't think it would be right for us to dump him in a nursing home. I would've felt like we'd sent him back to prison. Only problem: Lifecare Plus, the company Joe worked for, stopped sending female nurses a couple years back. Our dad often called them *Caroline*, which was okay, but he also sometimes said *Angie* and tried to grope them.

"Just stretching," I said, deciding not to mention Joe who Pop wouldn't recognize even after two years.

We walked a little farther, and he asked, "Where we going, Son?"

"Just taking a walk, Pop...."

———— • ♦ • ————

I'm not sure how Ted did it. He knew the right people in the right places, I guess. Somehow, he found Pop's mugshot from half a century ago. He had it blown up into a black and white eight-by-ten, then framed it. When he showed me, I stared at the picture and couldn't speak. There was Pop: Conway Jeffers, age

23, square-jawed and with a head full of dark hair parted neatly on the left. The height marker showed him to be five-nine.

Ted and I talked it over, and we agreed the picture would make a good gift for Pop on his seventy-fifth birthday. This was eighteen years after Mom died, and Pop's Alzheimer's had begun its long work of erasure. Pop talked openly about the murder now, sometimes regretting, other times swearing, *The son of a bitch had it comin'.* He told us he called the cops himself and confessed to it, his statement all true except for that one fib about Jimbo threatening to murder him first. He described the feel of the handcuffs—like a beartrap closing too slowly—and how he thought about his mama on the way to jail, wondering if she'd ever speak to him again because she was, as he put it, *scared of Jesus.* So, we thought it would be a fun thing to do for Pop to show him this image he swore he'd never seen. Maybe it was a bit tasteless, but at this point Pop seemed beyond worrying about stuff like that.

Ted and I arrived together, he in his expensive lawyer suit, I in my JCPenney classic. Pop met us at the door, his mind still clear enough to remember us and that it was his birthday, although not which one. He hugged us, accepted our gift, unwrapped it, stared at the picture for maybe three seconds, then removed it from its frame and walked away.

We followed him into the kitchen, each of us asking Pop if he was okay.

He didn't answer. His hand went into a drawer and came back holding a long, slender grill ignitor. He clicked it and touched the tiny flame to his picture.

"Sorry, Pop," Ted told him.

I said, "We thought you'd enjoy seeing it."

Pop waited until all but a corner burned away, then dropped the rest on the pale green linoleum and stomped on it. He bowed his head while we stood there in silence. After a while, he glanced up, met Ted's gaze, then mine, and said, "Boys, I'm never going back. They wanna catch me, least they won't have that to identify me with. I'm only a free man until the cops figure out they made a mistake in ever letting me go."

———— • ♦ • ————

Guiding Pop back around to the front yard, I stared through the fence at the dirt road and the creek beyond. Past that were more trees and hillsides, one of which was home to an overgrown cemetery. I could see a few tombstones sticking up through years of leaves and vines as if wanting to escape but held back by force.

He tapped me on the shoulder with the back of his hand. "Look," he said.

"What is it?"

He pointed. "Bull dug under the fence again."

"Sure, Pop. Sure." I almost asked him if he dug that hole himself. But I knew he wouldn't answer. Convicts know how to keep their secrets, sometimes even from themselves.

———— • ♦ • ————

AMERICAN TOAD

FOLKS IN CHARLESTON CALLED it frog-pocalypse, because that was the trendy thing to do. It toyed with a notion of the zombie apocalypse from popular culture so that everything became apocalyptic in the same way Watergate morphed into Contra-gate, Cattle-gate, Bridge-gate, and a hundred other -gates as if the word were a natural suffix. We'd already been through the aqua-pocalypse: a chemical leak soured all drinking water with the sweet stink of licorice—no one could swallow it or bathe in it for weeks. Then there was snow-pocalypse, when two feet of the white stuff fell—a lot even for our hilly part of the world. Now it was frogs. Well, American toads, actually. Thousands of them. Hundreds of thousands. Grayish brown with hints of emeralds and rust, they covered the trees like armored squirrels and dotted gardens and lawns like rocks. The air smelled like dead fish and cat piss. We were blighted, plagued. I half-expected to see Charlton Heston standing in the road, holding a stick, and roaring, "Let my people go!" But this was West Virginia, and we were no one's chosen.

Nobody really knew what caused the mass arrival of toads. There were theories, of course. We heard them every night on the news, put forth by goofy meteorologists trying to straddle the line between sarcasm and seriousness. Most said our bitterly cold winter broke open the back roads in too many places to fix, after which our rainy spring filled in the potholes with water. Those pools of murk then became breeding grounds for frogs and mosquitoes. If so, it was probably mosquito-pocalypse, too, although folks didn't hang around outside long enough to test that notion. We watched through our windows as the ground seemed to ooze like a lava lamp.

If we did go out, we never dared to step through a doorway without using a foot to brush the path. Toads were all over the place, and stepping on one felt like squashing a rotten tomato—a tomato that let out tiny shrieks like the sounds of mice in the walls.

Almost everyone in town stayed home. The city had been shut down. Restaurants and convenience stores remained closed. Even the two nearest Walmart superstores kept their doors locked, their parking lots empty. To look out our back window at the view across the river, we saw most streets bare except for freckles that moved. Candy and I were shut in, too. We didn't trust the driving conditions. Plus, how many dead toads would it take to destroy the engine of a BMW, to clog up the belts and pipes with guts?

In some ways, we were lucky. We had plenty of food, enough bottled water and sodas, a surplus of K-cups for the Keurig, liquor and beer left over from our last shindig, and even a backup generator should the power go out, although one of us would have to ford the river of amphibians to get to it and crank it up.

We weren't so fortunate in one regard: after the third day of the frog-pocalypse, Candy's prescription of Oxycontin ran out. Just a few weeks from her last treatment, she still felt horrible pain in her back and shoulders where the tumors had been. These agonies grew tenfold on the first day after her last pill. By noon, she had a look in her eyes that swore, *I'll kill you, you son of a bitch*, as if the toads were my fault, as if I'd conjured them just to make her suffer. Her eyes went dark with rage. I could swear her vivid amethysts turned to coal.

Come dinnertime, Candy was shaking and sweating. She couldn't eat. She sipped from a bottle of water, but soon hunched over the toilet, heaving up clear fluid.

I did what I could, spending much of the day trying to reach her oncologist. I left several messages with his answering service. A different woman answered each time and promised she'd have Dr. Richland call me back as soon as possible. He didn't. The toads kept him at home, too, I imagine, and apparently were so bad where he lived that they forcefully prevented him from punching numbers on his phone. Not that it mattered. I knew he couldn't just dial up the pharmacy—if one happened to be open—and demand, "Give Candace Hart some Oxycontin!" No, not with a strong drug like that. Those prescriptions had to be hand-written, which meant I'd need to meet him somewhere to collect the note. I was willing to make the effort, although the BMW'd never be the same.

That night, Candy didn't sleep. She shivered and groaned, sweating through the sheets despite her skin's clammy chill. A few times, I thought I heard her breathing slow. Even then, it lasted only moments before she was up and out of bed, running toward the bathroom. After Candy closed the door, the vomiting and diarrhea sounded identical.

I must have drifted off about three a.m., the last time I remembered looking at the clock. It felt weird how relaxed I was. The out-of-sync squawking of the toads soothed me like one of those nature soundtracks that's supposed to help you sleep. Toad songs did the trick, unlike the usual heavy metal concerts put on nightly by crickets or cicadas—which, come to think of it, I hadn't heard since the frog-pocalypse began.

In the morning, I awoke to discover Candy's side of the bed empty. I patted it to be sure, as if my eyes often lied. Then I got up and went to look for her. I found her on the living-room floor. She was naked and curled up on her side, her body squirming and making slow circles on the beige carpet. I saw the fresh spikelets of brown hair rising from her scalp like early wheat. Her fiery reddish-orange wig had slipped down. She held it to her face and sobbed into it.

I went to my knees and pressed a hand to her bare back.

She flinched.

"Candy, honey...."

Her wig muffled the sound of a scream. Her fists clenched, squeezing the fake hair as if trying to rip it apart.

"Baby, come up out of the floor. Let me help you."

She wailed something through her wig. It sounded like "Duck glue!"

"I'm trying, baby. Tell me what to do."

She pulled the wig away, revealing equally red cheeks, damp and swollen. "Make it stop," she groaned, before smothering herself again with her disguise.

"I will," I said. I meant it. I would. But how?

I tried the doctor again. This time, even his answering service didn't pick up. No voicemail, either. The line rang until I ended the call.

Stepping into the study, I slipped my iPhone in a back pocket of my cargo shorts, then rubbed my forehead with two fingers, fighting off a headache and hoping I could force myself to think. Think!

The answer—could it be that simple?—slapped me like a splash of cold water. Candy needed her medicine. I still had her medicine. Not the strong stuff she'd been taking, sure ... but something. She'd gone through several different drugs before Dr. Richland switched her to Oxycontin. Some of the pills made her sick. Others didn't help as the pain intensified. When he wrote the first script for Oxycontin, Dr. Richland sighed as if the act were distasteful to him, or as if it were inevitable. His gray pyramid eyebrows seemed to sag. He told me to make sure she didn't abuse the drugs, which I agreed to do. He also demanded that I dispose of all her other pills. He said he didn't want her to mix medications or accidentally overdose. I promised him that I would, then assured Candy that I had. Yet I kept them—for what purpose, I'm not sure—then forgot about them until now.

I went to the closet, opened the door, and dropped to my knees. The pill bottles were buried under worn towels and rags in an old white leather bag that once carried my grandfather's bowling ball to his weekly game. My dad claimed it after his papa died. It was beaten up and cracked, brown veins streaking the leather with a fishnet pattern. Dad never used it for anything. He stashed it on a shelf in his garage. Two years ago, I asked him why he kept it, and he said, "You're right. It's yours. You take it." Now I knew the answer to my question. He kept it for the same reasons I did: no one would want the bag, and it felt somehow wrong to throw it away.

Sifting through the towels, I dug out five bottles. One was green, the other four amber. I read the label on the green one: Tramadol. I doubted that would help. The pills in the first amber bottle I recognized as a nausea medicine. That might be useful, but it wouldn't solve the problem. Then there was an antibiotic. I twisted off the lid and counted half a dozen bi-colored capsules, wondering why she hadn't taken those. Resealing the bottle, I moved on to the other two. The label on the first read MS Contin, the second oxycodone/acetaminophen.

"Jackpot!" I said, my voice echoing in the mostly empty closet. "But which one?" One had Oxy in its name, and the other had Contin. "Half and half," I muttered. "Well, one of them better work." I kept these two and slid the other three back into my grandfather's bag, which I then replaced in the closet.

———— • ♦ • ————

Back in the living room, I squatted down next to Candy, balancing on the balls of my feet. I put my hand over the blue, black, and red snake tattooed on the pit of her back. "Hey."

She startled, moaned, slid on her belly like a snake herself.

"Candy," I said.

Candy groaned.

"Candy, look."

She turned her head slightly, lowering the wig. When she saw the amber bottles, she swung the rest of her body around. Her breasts were red from pressing against the carpet, her stomach streaked and lined like my grandfather's bag. "Where did you...?"

"I held on to these. Who knows, maybe one will help."

She sat up, leaving her red wig as a wet blob splashed across the floor. She took my hands in hers as if afraid to touch the bottles herself. She read the labels and said, "This one," tugging at my left hand. It was the one that read oxycodone/acetaminophen. "It's the same thing, just weaker. It's not meant to last as long."

Pulling my hands away, I finished reading the label. The dose read 10/325 mg. I unscrewed the cap. There were fifteen to twenty oblong white tablets inside. "How many?"

"Two," she said. "No, three. I need them to work fast."

I gave her what she wanted and watched as she swallowed the pills without water, grimacing and gagging only for a second. Immediately, she calmed, smiling. I knew the pain and trembling hadn't gone away, but it seemed as though just her knowing they would was enough to soothe her.

Candy leaned forward and wrapped her arms around my knee, squeezing. One of her nipples rubbed against my hairy calf. The sprouts on her scalp came up and jabbed at my chin.

I couldn't maintain my balance in the squat, so I dropped to the floor and held her back.

She said, "Jim, I didn't want you to see me like this."

"I didn't," I promised. "I was never here."

"Thank you," she said. "I guess I should find some clothes."

"Why bother?" I whispered, figuring the toads would keep guests away.

"Manners," she replied.

I couldn't tell if she meant hers or mine.

———— • ♦ • ————

The cable and internet went out around noon, but both came back a couple hours later. Which part bothered me more, I wondered. Was it the thought of being trapped here for days with nothing to dull my brain but liquor and nothing to stare at but the outside world through a window while American toads sometimes stared back in at me? Or was it the mental gore as I imagined rows of cable trucks roaming the city, crushing everything in sight as if giant feet tapdancing over bubble wrap and paintball pellets? Boredom plays tricks with the brain, but the mind knows what it knows.

I soon slipped back into the fog of forgetting once the constant coverage of frog-pocalypse resumed on the local news. I slumped back in my cyan recliner and watched as the balding weatherman joked about Armageddon. He pointed at a map of West Virginia depicting the expected path the toads would take as if they were an inland hurricane. Two days ago, the affected area had been one big blob of red over central and southern parts of the state. Now that red fanned southward, thinning and spreading like the radiation pattern after a nuclear accident.

Oh, I loved this stuff. I could sit here watching disaster coverage for days. It was like after the Towers fell. The lone thing that could satiate my hollowness was a constant filling with information, however awful it might be. It's something I picked up while working at the dealership. During dead times between customers, I'd stare at one of the four giant screens carefully placed around the showroom. Whenever calamity happened, I saturated my cells with news. I watched CNN, where the reporters, in their haste to tell the story first, often got the facts wrong, only to correct them later. I stood mesmerized by Fox News, where the truth came out, and then the reporters got the story wrong. I savored the tasty morsels offered up by MSNBC, where everything was a joke told in deadpan voice, and even the dry spectacle of CSPAN, where a few jokes would've been welcome.

The local news flashed back to the anchor's desk. A blue-suited, silver-haired robot was asking questions of a young female staffer from the mayor's office. Her Skyped face cut in and out, replaced momentarily by a black screen.

"...coffee grounds...," she was saying. "...in your garden. Scatter ... your house."

"Will that kill them or drive them off?" the anchorman asked.

"...just a theory. We don't..."

"Lovely," I muttered, looking over my shoulder at the Keurig on the kitchen counter. There'd be no scattering of coffee grounds for us. Technology had eliminated that suddenly useful waste, replacing it with plastic pods good for even less.

I caught movement out of the corner of my eye. I turned toward the window and saw an American toad staring back at me from the other side of the glass. An outline of my own pale, squared-off head reflected also, superimposed above the toad's. The amphibian's glossy beads of eyes became mine, forming a new creature that resembled the caricature of Edgar Allan Poe I'd seen on goofy tee shirts.

"Go away," I said, not sure if I meant the words for me, the toad, or the hideous monster made of both.

The young woman had moved on to listing the pros and cons of spraying the roads with citric acid (it didn't sound promising or a likely option) when my doorbell chimed. The hollow four-note pattern—dum dee dee dum—startled me out of my chair.

Who the hell would come over at a time like this? Would the act be considered stupid or brave? Unnecessary, certainly, and unexpected.

I moved quickly toward the door, stubbing my little toe on the corner of the coffee table.

"Shit!" I cried.

"Was that the door?" Candy shouted from our bedroom.

"I got it," I yelled back. I shook my foot, trying to stop the pain, then reached for the knob. I didn't bother to look through the peephole. I doubted there were Jehovah's witnesses or political hucksters going door to door on a day like this. Instead, I expected to see something like that scene in *The Exorcist* where the old priest first looks up at the house with a sense of foreboding. It might have been that, too, if Max von Sydow were dressed like Bozo the Clown. I inched the door back just a bit while I stared down to make sure no American toads slipped through the crack. As such, the first thing I saw was a pair of brown high-top canvas shoes, followed by lime-green socks into which the legs of khaki pants were tucked. I knew who it was before my eyes reached the plaid vest, an odd combination of colors that seemed to match the American Toads all around us, constricting over a white dress shirt or the fat face adjoining half a neck. The blond eyebrows and circular pattern of thinning blond hair filled out the portrait. "Morris, are you out of your mind?"

"Hey, Jim," he said. "Just checking on everybody." His high voice cracked with mirth. "Mind if I come in? It's frog-pocalypse out here, you know." He kicked a toad off the doorstep.

"Sure, sure," I said, stepping back. I opened up, urging Morris Vandevander through the gap. I slammed the door as soon as he was clear.

Morris owned the monuments store over on Lee Street. A widower with six absent adult daughters, Morris headed our neighborhood watch and felt it was his civic duty to mind everyone's business. He sent out mass e-mails with subject lines like *Someone stole the spare change out of the Johnsons' car last night* or *Two teens seen running up Slack Road at 4 a.m.* I once imagined him sitting by his living-room window, permanently propped in a chair like Norman Bates's mother. Sure, it was good to have someone on our side, keeping an eye out for criminals and such, but I thought Morris went too far. Recently, he passed around a petition to have lights installed near the ruins of an old Civil War fort. Morris said kids were up there drinking and screwing at all hours of the night, which was probably what kids had been doing since the Civil War ended. I wanted no part of that petition.

I shook my head, erasing the bad thoughts. "Would you like a cup of coffee, Morris? Maybe a bourbon?"

"Appreciate it, but no. I'm just checking on folks. Making sure you have supplies."

"We're good," I said. "Ask us again in a week ... if this craziness lasts that long."

Morris grimaced. "No siree," he said. "I saw on the boob tube that the experts think our world's calming down by the weekend. The frog population's already starting to dwindle."

"Toads," I said.

"What's that?"

"Never mind." I urged him to follow me into the living room, where the TV still buzzed. The anchorman was interviewing a local pastor about the toads, Bible prophecies, spiritual preparedness, and the like. I didn't need to hear any more of that conversation, so I grabbed the remote and pushed OFF.

"I don't mean to interrupt you, Jim. Glad to see you're okay. How's the missus?"

As soon as he asked the question, I heard Candy's voice behind me. "Morris? Is that you?" I turned and saw her coming down the hallway. She'd changed into a blue satin blouse and a pair of loose-fitting jeans. She wore a sandy-blond wig in a style that reminded me of early David Bowie. The color had returned to her cheeks, and she was smiling. She had a glaze to her eyes so slight that I doubt Morris noticed. I wouldn't have noticed either if I hadn't witnessed the way her eyes looked earlier when that glaze wasn't there.

"Candace, honey, how you feeling?"

"Never better," she lied. She went toward him and gave Morris a hug. Her thin arms around his thick body resembled netting trying to hold a ham hock together.

"Ain't you just the sweetest," he said. "Jim treating you all right?"

"Never better," she repeated, and this time I could tell she meant it.

The hug was growing uncomfortable for Morris. Candy held on too long, and I noticed that Morris didn't hug her back. He held his arms at his sides as if afraid to place a hand against her skin. It was as if he worried how it might look. He had a thing for her, I realized. He didn't want me to see his hunger, but gave it away by resisting. We'd known Morris for about five years. He'd been to our house a hundred times. We fixed dinner for him and his wife Jennifer when she was still alive. How long had he been lusting after Candy?

Sweet Jesus, I thought. Maybe she wanted him, too. He was her type: short, out of shape, and still handsome in that 90s-Jack-Nicholson sort of way. It could be that they would've had an affair if not for the cancer. Was that likely? Was it a real thing or just in my imagination? Did that mean I should love her cancer and sing its praises?

Again, I shook my head. "How's the tombstone business?" I asked, just to say something.

Morris seemed happy for the distraction. As Candy backed away from him, he said, "Slow couple of weeks." He laughed as if hearing a joke in his head. He tried to vocalize it. "People don't even want to die until the frogs are gone. It's like they're afraid to leave too soon and miss the Rapture." His chortles croaked like a smoker's cough.

"I like your socks," Candy told him.

Morris blushed. "Thanks. My littlest darling bought them." His littlest darling, Llewellyn, was twenty-seven and living in Kentucky.

I went to the bar and poured myself a bourbon, skipping the ice and soda. "Sure you don't want one, Morris?"

He squinted as he considered it. "No, thanks. I better get on my way. Still have other folks to check on, you know."

"Of course."

"Oh, don't leave yet," Candy mock-whined.

"Sorry, Candace, honey. I really need to make tracks." He looked down and paused as if checking to be sure his pants remained neatly tucked into his socks.

I swallowed the burn of warm bourbon. It went down so fast that I couldn't taste the Early Times.

"I'm glad you two are all right."

I stifled a laugh. *Except for my wife's cancer, drug problem, and surprising interest in you,* I thought. "Except for the toads," I said, setting down my glass and escorting Morris to the door.

"Yeah, except for them," he finally said as if coming out of a trance. "Well, take care. I'll see you when I see you." He opened the door and walked out carelessly. I expected to hear the squish and squeal.

I stepped in to fill the gap, but hesitated. Staring up at me from the doorstep was a fat American toad, its eyes bulging, skin gray-brown and lumpy. For all I knew, it could've been the one from the windowsill earlier. Improbable, sure, but nothing felt normal to me now. I wanted to get back to selling sports cars, being on top of my game in the battle of wills it took to convince people they should buy luxury items they didn't really need. I enjoyed pushing them over the edge, guiding them, making their decisions for them. At times like that, I felt whole. I never worried about cancer, toads, or horny neighbors on the prowl. I never worried which kinds of pills would fix my wife.

"Go on home," I said to the toad.

Halfway up the road, Morris offered a backhanded wave.

COLORFUL ALIENS

HE KEPT HIS HEAD down, never made eye contact, walked with a purpose as though he were following a trail of breadcrumbs through the city. His feet moved in rhythm like Ping-Pong paddles as if Charlie were a clarinetist marching in some holiday parade. Each brown shoe entered and then left his vision. It helped him ignore gray of the sky and gray of the streets, not to mention gray of other pedestrians on their way to work, coffee shops, or a life of petty crime.

Charlie didn't look up when the blue blur barred his way, but tried to sidestep around it. His glossy Florsheims slid right then, still impeded, went left again. If only the two brown boulders that looked like work boots hadn't stepped along with them, Charlie might not have heard that deep, god-like voice demand, "Let me see your wallet."

Charlie stopped, dazed by the interruption and already trembling as the adrenaline hit. When Charlie raised his eyes, he saw a man so tall that his head would've struck the awning in front of most of the downtown restaurants. The guy was dark-eyed and dark-skinned, wearing a midnight blue toboggan and matching full-length coat trimmed in wool the color of beach sand. His arm was bent at the elbow, gloved hand the size of a satellite dish stretched toward Charlie.

"Are you robbing me?" said Charlie, a crackle of panic in his voice.

"Wouldn't do that," bellowed the giant. "Raised better. Now let me see your wallet."

Charlie wasn't convinced. Not that it mattered. Whether from fear he was being mugged or relief that he wasn't, Charlie reached into his back pocket, pulling out that worn, leather lump. "You're sure you're not robbing me?" he said.

"I told you, my mama raised me better."

"Then why am I giving you my wallet?"

"Trust me, when you see this, you'll *want* to give me money—gladly, and with an enchanted heart." He snatched the wallet from Charlie's hands before the words could register. Flipping it open, he stayed away from the cash and credit cards, pausing to glance at Charlie's driver's license. "Charles Knoll," he said. "Wasn't there a guy...?"

That irritated Charlie more than being robbed. "Yes," he said. "Yes there was."

"I mean the guy who...."

"Yes, yes."

"Were you...?"

"Good lord." Charlie shook his head. "My dad was a big fan. Can we get on with it?"

"Sorry," the giant moaned. It wasn't a word that sounded right coming from one so large he could get away with offending almost anybody. He bowed his head, frozen breath creeping around his cheeks like a beard. His thumb the size of a pistol shot through the plastic sleeves, a few of which carried photographs. He stopped when he found a picture he liked. "This your wife?"

Charlie tilted in to look. The picture was of a young brunette, wide-eyed and still skinny, a smile breaking in mixed directions on her lips. She wore lipstick the color of bubblegum, and Charlie almost thought he could smell the apple scent of her perfume, although when his subconscious tricked him into trying, his nostrils froze from the sterile winter air. "That's her," he said. "Old picture, but it's her."

"Perfect, Chuck," said the giant.

"It's Charlie. Don't call me Chuck."

"Oh, I see. Well, Charlie, if you'd be so kind, pull that photo out. My hands are a little ... well, clumsy. I'd end up tearing the plastic."

"Why would I...?"

"Trust me, Charlie. The Great Mondo never does anything without a reason." He paused. "Besides, you can have your wallet back."

Charlie still felt the urge to turn and run. He glanced up, trying to judge intent in the big man's eyes, but vertigo hit him as if he were watching a meteor shower while standing. Shaking it off, he muttered, "Sure, sure, whatever," and did as he was told.

Then, happy to have his wallet back, he squeezed it like a stress ball or a pair of adjustable pliers.

Mondo laughed like a barking seal. "I promise you, Charlie, this is magic like you've never seen." He rubbed the photo between his hands. It vanished, its corners reappeared here and there like the wings of crows flying through a choppy mist.

Charlie thought that might be the whole trick. Maybe Mondo wasn't a street magician at all, but just some lunatic. "Okay," he said. "And?"

"You watching?"

"Sure," said Charlie.

"Watching close?"

"Yeah, whatever."

The Great Mondo bowed his head and blew on his hands. He said something that sounded like, "*Shabbadabba.*" Then he straightened up and continued rubbing the photo. Now, corners were visible at the same time on both the thumb and pinky sides of his hands, with a third point sticking out near the middle fingers. Mondo kept rubbing, and the photo appeared to stretch. "You see?" he said. "Magic."

Charlie admitted it was a neat illusion, but not too complicated. He figured Mondo carried a larger photo up his sleeve. Those sleeves, after all, could make footballs disappear. Charlie said as much.

Mondo seal-laughed again. "Don't be so closed-minded, my friend. Here, see for yourself." He stopped rubbing and handed over the picture.

Charlie took it and stared. It was the same picture, but several times its normal size. *This is no illusion*, he thought. It was his picture, all right. It showed his wife back when he still loved her and she still cared how she looked. But the snapshot was so much larger now. Charlie wondered if what the big man had up his sleeve was a scanner with a photo printer attached. "My God," he said. "How...?"

"Worth your time?" said Mondo.

Charlie didn't reply. As he stared at the picture, it still seemed to be growing.

"Worth a few bucks, maybe? I can tell you're amused, amazed, a man in need of a little myth and wonder."

Without answering, Charlie opened his billfold and fished out two fives, handing them over.

"Thank you, my friend whose father was a big fan of a big man. I appreciate the contribution."

Charlie looked up. "I'll give you another ten if you can make it small again. I can't fit it back in my wallet like this."

— • ♦ • —

Charlie reached for the front door to the building where he worked and noticed his reflection in the glass. *That's not me*, he thought. He looked older than he remembered, heavier and sagging in the cheeks. His hair showed early streaks of gray at the temples. His head slouched forward on his neck. The only life was in his eyes, stretched wide in awe, two black holes in the center sucking all the light into them.

Disoriented, he tugged at the door's metal handle. It seemed different, too: larger, crooked, a bit too warm. Everything around him was out of proportion with what he remembered. He glanced up, and the twenty stories bulged and leaned as if they might topple and crush him.

Charlie shook his head and went inside where the yellow-tinted lobby stretched for miles like in a dream. The people there were all giants to him. Towering in their grays and blacks, they leered down, huffing at him as if he were a child scattering his toys across the floor.

Shielding his eyes, Charlie raced for the elevator.

"What level?" someone asked.

"Seventeen," Charlie muttered. Around him, the wide, barren world from steel wall to steel wall spun like a carnival ride.

"Hello, Charlie."

"Morning, Mr. Knoll."

"How's it going, Charlie?"

He mumbled his hellos and hurried through to his office, closing the door behind him. How he despised these people, he thought. They had become a part of his life like warts that never quite burned off. He considered them friends once. Now, they haunted him with their fake smiles and feigned care for his wellbeing. They had become a part of his routine like reading the morning memos, phone messages, and e-mails. He ignored them as much as possible during the day and forgot them altogether when he made it home.

Home. It was where he spent those hours of erasure, flipping back and forth between news channels and the endless cop and reality shows that filled all the networks every night. Charlie liked to see what was going on in the world ... so he could complain about, or fear it. He dreaded the next terror attack, the next school shooting, home invasion, or electrical fire that killed a family of five while everyone slept. He resented the politicians—the current President most of all, except perhaps the previous one. Each night there was another celebrity scandal, a corporate scandal, a sports cheating scandal. He hated all of it and found what little joy he knew in hating. And those TV shows? Best not to think of them, because all they were good for was helping him not to think.

How did he get this way? he wondered. How did so much sediment settle in his bones? He was an average lawyer at an average firm. He put in an average day's work, then went home to an average wife that rarely noticed him. She came home from her shift at the hospital and either took a long nap or locked herself in her room and scrolled through Facebook on the computer. Sometimes, he hoped she was in there having cybersex with a stranger. At least that would make her life more interesting. His, too, if she ever came clean.

It hadn't always been like that. Charlie often thought about when they met. He was in law school, and she worked in the emergency room where he ended up after a minor wreck. She had tight, pale skin that smelled of green apples and sterile soap. Her brown hair was tied off in back. She wore a maroon uniform that hid her shape, with a nametag over her breast that read, *Bacall*. Having a famous name himself, he asked the obvious question, and she replied, "No, it's Wendy." Then she touched the back of her hand to his forehead as if checking for a fever. From that first touch, he loved her.

The walls of his office pulsed like a cow's heart, their fleshy panels stretching in and pulling out. He felt their movement in his temples as if sharing the rhythm. He squeezed his forehead with his hands and said, "Stop it, stop it, stop it!"

The walls, as if compromising, settled into a steadier pattern like his wife's chest while she slept. How he loved to watch her then—hair tangled, face red from the press of a pillow. He listened for her breath and those slight groans she made as though she had a lover with her on the other side. He liked to whisper her name, too. "Wendy," he'd say, knowing her dream self would mutter something incomprehensible in reply.

"Mr. Knoll?"

Charlie jerked, startled. He hadn't heard Kylie Kurtz, one of the interns, enter the room. He stared dumbly at the blond halo around her wind-burned face.

"I didn't mean to bother you."

"It's okay. Just a headache. A migraine, I think."

He expected her to ask, "Are you all right?" or, "Is there something I can get you?" Instead, she told him, "Mr. Eberton said to bring this to you." She waved a file folder that must have held a thousand pages. It kept growing, and Charlie didn't understand how she managed to hold onto it. "It's the settlement offer on Boniver. They've put it in writing. Mr. Eberton wants you to take a look at it and let him know what you think." The Boniver case was a simple nursing home suit. The defendants had offered a quarter of a million with a nondisclosure clause to settle. The document shouldn't have been more than a handful of pages, but the file was as fat as a shoebox now, fleshy and thrashing about like an infant. Kylie's fingers were stretched almost to a straight line.

"For God's sake," Charlie snapped, "set it on my desk before you hurt yourself!"

She flinched as if she had seen her dead mother's face through a window. Stepping farther into the room, she tossed the file. It landed with a booming whump like a spray can exploding.

Charlie grabbed his forehead again. He paid no attention as Kylie Kurtz fled the room.

———— • ♦ • ————

He came to on the floor, his face pressed against the thin, gray carpet. His arms felt numb and limp beneath him.

Someone cried out—maybe Kylie, though he couldn't be sure.

Someone else said, "Call nine-one-one." That voice, he recognized as belonging to Janice Jarvis, the office manager.

"No," he grunted, rolling over onto his side. Everything looked fuzzy at first as if covered with dust, but his eyes adjusted. "I'm fine. Really." Four people were in the room with him. He could make them out now: Kylie and Janice, but also Ron Chandler and Lisa West, two of the associates. Charlie saw them staring down at him, their eyelids compressed into a lawyerly show of concern.

"It's okay," he said. "I'm fine. No ambulance. Give me a sec to get my bearings."

"What's going on? Let me through." It was a bass voice, rumbling like a flat tire. Mr. Finback, the senior partner, bulled his way into the room. He wore a charcoal suit, menacing and austere. "Knoll," he said, going to one knee and placing a meaty pink hand on Charlie's shoulder, "what happened here? You drunk? On drugs? What's the matter?"

"No, sir. Just had a...."

"What?"

"Dizzy spell, I guess."

"Are you sick?" the old man asked. Charlie could smell the heavy track of English Leather on his skin.

"I don't think so. I mean, no. Maybe my sugar's off." He started to say that maybe *everything* was off, but he realized just before the words came out that the room wasn't pulsing or spinning anymore. The walls weren't fifty feet high, and the people looked like people again. He blinked, squinted, and stared up at Mr. Finback's silver-trimmed rosy face. No part of the old man was any different than Charlie remembered.

"What is it, Knoll? Why are you staring at me like that?"

"Sorry, sir," said Charlie. "Really, I'm fine. If I could just...." He pushed against the floor with his tingling hands.

"Sure, sure," said the old lawyer. He slid an arm under Charlie's and, with a tug, helped him to his feet. "Maybe you should take the rest of the day off, Knoll. Go home. Get some sleep."

"Thank you, but I'm fine," said Charlie. And he was. All the cubist renderings of the world around him had switched to a more realist tone. "I think I just need to put some food in my belly. That should do the trick. If you don't mind, I think I'll go to lunch."

Mr. Finback scowled and checked his watch. "Go on, then. Just call us and let us know if you have another episode."

⸻ • ♦ • ⸻

He sat at a red table by the window in back. Everywhere he looked, men and women lumbered like zombies, holding their trays at arms' length like convicts. Voices were raised. Crumbs from biscuits fell to the floor. A teenager in a camouflage coat slid his tray through the swinging cat door above the wastebasket, knocking over a half-full soda that spilled in a flood.

Charlie tried to ignore the chaos and focus on his Egg McMuffin. He had taken two bites. The rest lay in front of him like a balled-up sock someone had tossed aside. He wondered why his perspective couldn't be off *now*. His meal might look gigantic, juicy and appealing. Not that he was hungry. Not at ten o'clock in the morning.

Before, Charlie felt disoriented and strange. It was as though someone picked him up and placed him inside a videogame—one of the old Atari versions where everything was squared off, larger than life, and full of colorful aliens. At the moment though, all had returned to normal, and he understood how lousy normal was, how much he despised it. Normal was greasy breakfast sandwiches and affectless lawyers jabbering about their interrogatories and motions to dismiss. It was gray buildings and grayer streets, while he loped along the gray sidewalks afraid to look around or meet the gray eyes of any stranger. Then it was going home to an overpriced apartment he lived in with a wife that rarely knew he was there. Both had grown round, both prematurely gray in streaks. They didn't argue, but they also didn't discuss politics, the Academy Awards, the war in Iraq—when there was one—or the jokes on late-night TV that were funny even when they didn't make a lot of sense. Charlie felt as though he and Wendy were just roommates, sharing space and not caring all that much when the other was around.

Again, he wondered how it happened. They had been so passionate at first: sneaking into public restrooms together, making out in the hospital's outdoor smoking area despite that neither of them smoked, talking on the phone all night so that both went to work most days with black bands around their eyes from lack of sleep. When did that change? Charlie wasn't sure. The scene that stuck in his mind happened a couple years after they married. He sat with Wendy on the couch, the two of them kissing, neither rushed, both ready. She gave him a nod he knew meant, *Let's go into the bedroom.* She stood, and he followed, loosening his tie. Then, just before Wendy reached the bedroom door, she turned to him and said, "Take your socks off this time." She hadn't said that to him before. It was a small thing, but the fact Wendy felt comfortable and unhurried enough to make such a request meant their relationship was different. Looking back, Charlie saw it as the start of the decline.

He pulled the egg square off his muffin and nibbled at a corner. It was cold and unappealing, a Eucharist he took in as though a miracle might happen. None ever did.

Charlie turned his head, staring out the window at cars in a slow-speed race along the avenue nearby. Conflicting crowds marched east and west, blocking his view. Sometimes the waves broke, and he saw a splash of blue like a bird's egg hidden among the branches of a dead tree. *That looks familiar*, he thought. It was a blue, wool-lined, full-length coat big enough to bury a couple of bodies in.

"You," said Charlie. He stood, leaving his tray and half-uneaten muffin on the table, and headed for the door. He had seen the big man out back, so he had to walk around the building. His heart raced as if he were infatuated, or as if he were about to be shot. Coldness filled his gut. A nerve twitched and fluttered in his left shoulder. Charlie gasped for air as if drowning rather than just out of shape. Maneuvering through the pedestrians as if they were cars, he took care not to hit or be hit by them.

The Great Mondo sat on a steel bench, facing the avenue. A McDonalds bag lay beside him, its top rolled down as far as it would go. Mondo didn't wear his toboggan now, and mist rose from his bald head like breath in the winter air. It looked like a magician's trick, and Charlie thought for a moment that Mondo might disappear. Moving closer, he heard the big man humming.

Charlie sat down on the edge of the bench. He didn't say anything at first, but stared ahead at slow-moving cars. His ears tingled from the cold, as did the tip of his nose. It went on like that for a minute or two—Charlie staring, Mondo humming—before the lawyer grew anxious and spoke. "You're not a magician at all, are you?"

Mondo's hums turned into seal-like laughter.

"I mean, there was a trick all right, but it wasn't magic."

"How's that?"

"Not an illusion."

"You think so?"

"No sleight of hand, hocus pocus, abracadabra."

Mondo brought back his cough of a laugh. "I know you," he said. "Twenty bucks, right?"

"That's me," said Charlie.

"Named after the coach, but *don't call me Chuck*."

"You got it," said Charlie. "But I saw you and came to tell you I figured it out."

"So you say. What's to figure out?"

"You hypnotized me," Charlie told him, not criticizing but stating as if a well-known fact. "I thought it was a neat magic trick, but then you fixed it and the effects didn't wear off. My head was screwed up for an hour."

Mondo glanced at Charlie and then turned away. When he spoke, the deep bellow of his voice vanished. He sounded like any average guy Charlie might run into on the street. "I'm sorry, man. Didn't mean to leave you hazy. Just trying to make a few bucks, you know?"

The lawyer shook his head, his breath streaking the air. "Don't worry about it," he said. "I wanted to be sure. Mondo's not your real name, is it?"

"Raymond," said Mondo. He held out his massive right hand.

Charlie shook it as best he could, his cold, pale fingers almost disappearing. "Nice to meet you, Raymond."

"Likewise, man."

"So, you hypnotized me."

"Sure," said the Great Mondo.

"That takes some skill. You're pretty good."

"Good enough, I guess."

"What I want to know is, can you do it again?"

"You want me to...?"

"And do it, uh, on a little bigger scale. There's fifty bucks in it for you."

"I'm listening."

"The thing is.... Well...."

"What?" said Mondo.

"I want you to make me love my wife again."

Mondo was silent at first, but soon he slipped into his best Mondo voice, using it not for speech but for that heavy laughter. He roared wordlessly like a busted loudspeaker. White breaths hopped through the air like cartoon rabbits. He tried to get a few words out, but what needed said? The man wanted what he wanted, even if he didn't know he wanted it until now.

ABOUT RUNNING WILD PRESS

Running Wild Press publishes stories that cross genres with great stories and writing. RIZE publishes great genre stories written by people of color and by authors who identify with other marginalized groups. Our team consists of:

Lisa Diane Kastner, Founder and Executive Editor
Joelle Mitchell, Licensing and Strategy Lead
Cody Sisco, Acquisition Editor, RIZE
Benjamin White, Acquisition Editor, Running Wild
Peter A. Wright, Acquisition Editor, Running Wild
Resa Alboher, Editor
Angela Andrews, Editor
Sandra Bush, Editor
Ashley Crantas, Editor
Rebecca Dimyan, Editor
Abigail Efird, Editor
Aimee Hardy, Editor

Henry L. Herz, Editor
Cecilia Kennedy, Editor
Barbara Lockwood, Editor
AE Williams, Editor
Scott Schultz, Editor
Rod Gilley, Editor
Kelly Ottiano, Editor
Carolyn Banks, Editor

Evangeline Estropia, Product Manager
Pulp Art Studios, Cover Design
Standout Books, Interior Design
Polgarus Studios, Interior Design

Learn more about us and our stories at
www.runningwildpublishing.com

Loved this story and want more? Follow us at
www.runningwildpublishing.com/rize,
 www.facebook/runningwildpress,
on Twitter @lisadkastner @RunWildBooks

www.ingramcontent.com/pod-product-compliance
Lightning Source LLC
LaVergne TN
LVHW011934070526
838202LV00054B/4632